BEAUFORD PLACE

Written by

GWANDINE

COVER PAINTING BY

GWANDINE

Gwandine.com

WesternParables.com

Published by Faithful and Holy is He! Studios and Productions

ISBN-13: 978-0615847283
ISBN-10: 0615847285

LORD our Lord, how excellent is thy name in all the earth! Psalm 8:9

I dedicate this book to my Lord and Saviour Jesus Christ! Afterward, my mother, Ms. Barbara Thomas, all African-American cowboys and cowgirls past and present, and my blood descendants—the Brassfields of the Cherokee Nation.

Although Beauford Place is a work of fiction, numerous historical African-American cowboys participated in cattle drives and rodeos since the beginning of the cowboy era. They branded cattle, tamed wild horses, rode with Native-Americans, and accomplished numerous feats as they still do as there are present day African-American rodeo performers and real cowboys.

I pray that you enjoy this inspirational story of love and courage between an African-American cowboy and an austere lady.

Look for the unabridged audio version of this book narrated by the author. Enjoy over five hours of storytelling.

Visit: **WesternParables.com** or **TheBlackWest.com**

Live, love, laugh, lament, and luxuriate in literature!™

I enjoy painting African-American cowboys, their ladies, and Native-Americans in western scenery on canvas for my book covers. I am also the wife of a pastor and have two adult children. My husband is of Blackfoot Native-American descent.

Sometimes, people ask me the meaning of my name, Gwandine. My mother told me that my grandmother entreated her to name me Gwandine. The meaning is listed below and accurately describes me.

GWANDINE

Likes to have a fun time and a good laugh
Charming, romantic, and expressive
Is very gifted
Takes the oppressed to heart
Trusting-yet wise in all she does
A lady whose voice is music to the ears
Modest, noble, clever, and adroit
Is thrifty, determined, and a deep thinker

Chapter 1

Inspirational Historical Fiction
Beauford Place
Year: 1881

"Need any help ladies?"

The tall dark stranger dismounted his steed and stood facing Mary Ellen.

Her eyes were fixated upon the stranger clad in black cowboy attire. His clean-shaven face depicted smooth dark brown skin with deep brown eyes that seemed to twinkle as he smiled. His black leather gloves concealed his rough ranchman's hands. A black ten-gallon cowboy hat sat atop his head. He was dressed in black corduroy frontier pants that had a pocket watch compartment with a silver pocket watch enclosed and a brass compass attached to the waist.

His pants covered his black leather boots that draped slightly over his ankles. He wore a matching black corduroy weskit over a red long-sleeved shirt with a red neckerchief around his neck fastened with a silver slide.

Her eldest sister Mae smiled and introduced her. "Nate this is my little sister."

He gently lifted his cowboy hat and nodded. "So this is the long awaited *Little Stockings*. Heard a lot of good things about you Miss."

Mary Ellen's mind appeared to have vanished for a moment until Mae hunched her. "It's nice to uh—meet you."

Mae snickered while the young handsome cowboy displayed a generous smile. "It was nice meeting you Miss and welcome home."

Mary Ellen was taken by surprise, as he was not what she expected. She slowly regained her composure and was embarrassed at her nervousness. He mounted the steed, it reared forming a perfect silhouette with the sun as a backdrop, and then he rode toward the stables.

Mr. John carried her bags inside the mansion and when she entered a large group of people yelled, "Welcome home!" Mary Ellen's hand covered her mouth and then she popped Mae's head with her fingers. "Why didn't you tell me?"

Mae laughed and retorted, "Then it wouldn't have been a surprise, would it?"

"I suppose you're right."

Mama Mae approached her arrayed in a floor-length mauve dress. She's a large robust godly woman with a voice that's music to the ears. Her pressed hair was styled high on her head proudly displaying its grayish highlights. Mama Mae had recently received her new pressing comb through a mail-order catalog. If she had worn any of her stylish millinery, it would appear as if she was on her way to church. Mama Mae was the first to grab her as she smacked a huge wet kiss on her cheek. She was largely known for her wet kisses.

"Oh my baby's a college graduate," she rejoiced as the others began to express their accolades and appreciation for her accomplishment.

After everyone seemed to settle down, Mama Mae grabbed one of the uncles that had a camera. "Addison, we need to get a picture of Little Stockings."

Mary Ellen quickly interjected, "Mama please let me change and fix my hair. I'll be back as soon as I'm finished." She grabbed the sides of her skirt and scurried upstairs to her bedroom.

After slowly spinning around the room, she realized that everything was just as it was. The room contained her full-size bed that had a tall walnut headboard with ornately carved roses and a matching chest-of-drawers, vanity, and wardrobe.

Mary Ellen unlocked the double-doors, stepped out on her verandah, and looked down. She noticed Nathan busily assisting the other workers with the preparations. It became obvious to her that Mama Mae was preparing for a barbeque. Before she could step back inside her bedroom, Nathan glanced upward and caught a glimpse of her. She waved and he returned the gesture. A pleasant smile emerged on her face.

She could hear the excitement of their loud-talking family and friends. Everyone was jovial. Many of the church members were there as well as some that weren't saved. Those were the ones that would occasionally sneak off and take a little nip of their sour mash or corn liquor that they had slipped past Mama Mae's eyes. Had she known, her soprano voice would have resonated to an extremely loud shriek and not due to the law of the land. It was the law of the Beauford household.

Mary Ellen plopped down on her bed supine. Although she preferred to take a nap, she knew that wouldn't suffice. Mary Ellen reminisced on the earlier events of that morning as she prepared to freshen up and change her walking skirt suit. She reminded herself of the early morning events that occurred prior to her arrival home as the sound of the train and the conductor announcing the stations seemed to haunt her.

"*Tradassa Station!* We're approaching Tradassa Station," the conductor had announced. A crowd of onlookers stared down the tracks as they anxiously awaited the *Blue Gypsy* as its smoke billowed alerting everyone of its commanding presence. Exiting passengers vigorously forced their way through the crowd. Mary Ellen stepped down as she gripped the sides of her ankle-length burgundy skirt. She glanced around praying that someone would be there to take her home.

Finally, she eyed her sister Mae, known by the family as *Big Mae* who stood out amongst the crowd with her hands poised on her full-figured hips. Mary Ellen beckoned as she waved her arm and was relieved that Mae acknowledged her gesture. She bolted toward Mae.

"So how does it feel to be the first one to graduate from college in the family?"

Mary Ellen's smile outstretched everyone's because she's now Mary Ellen Beauford, Ph.D., which was a major accomplishment for their family and historically.

Unable to stop herself from grinning, she was speechless. She managed to squeeze out a response. "It feels grand—just grand!" She hugged Mae as best that she could.

"Let me look at you!"

Mary Ellen stepped back and was dressed in a walking jacket with a matching waist-fitted skirt, weskit, and lace gloves. Her Victorian style touring hat depicted fine millinery craftsmanship layered with ribbons, bows, and plumage. Concealed underneath was her long voluminous crinkly black tresses encircled in a bun, which made her astuteness obvious. Her burgundy walking suit absorbed sunrays that magnified her smooth coffee brown complexion.

"Daddy would be proud. I just know he would. I know he's somewhere smiling down on you knowing that his baby girl made it!"

Mary Ellen's warm brown eyes stared blankly at Mae.

"I'm not the first colored woman to graduate from college in this country. There was another before me. You know daddy wanted me to be the first to obtain my Ph.D."

Mae placed one of her arms around her little sister's shoulders. "I know. Let's get out of here and go see mama and Big Stockings; then you can tell us all about it. Mama saved all your letters you know."

Mary Ellen displayed a toothy grin. "I figured that she would."

Mae is the eldest and the most outspoken of the three sisters in the Beauford family named after their mother that everyone calls *Mama Mae*. Marva, known as *Big Stockings* is the middle sister of their family. Nonetheless, the youngest and most successful sister is Mary Ellen known as *Little Stockings*.

An older well-dressed gentleman greeted her with a polite smile. His eyes displayed the many years of wisdom that he possessed. "Welcome home Little Stockings."

She returned the smile. "It's good to see you again Mr. John." He assisted the ladies into their carriage and loaded the travel bags resembling those of a carpetbagger.

The Beauford family became wealthy due to their late father, Benjamin Beauford's invention of a mechanism that simplified farming. Benjamin expired while Mary Ellen was away at college. She never forgot the last time that she saw him alive. Mary Ellen always admired his strength and courage. But what she admired most is her memory of the many evenings they had spent sitting on the large front verandah when Benjamin shared his stories from when he was a young lad. He had spent many days imparting wisdom with hope that she would finish college and not fall into temptation and arrive home with child. That very thing happened to a daughter of a friend of his and he didn't want it to happen to her.

She couldn't help but wonder why her sisters never took advantage of their father's blessing. Unable to restrain herself any longer she blurted, "Why didn't you go to school?"

Her question took Mae by surprise. "'*Cause* I just don't want to. Besides, I'm too old and Jack wouldn't want me to go away."

Mary Ellen gave an eye roll. "You know full well that Jack only married you to get his foot in the Beauford family fortune!" It was then that Mary Ellen caught a glimpse of Mr. John's lips curl up in a smile as he quietly drove the carriage. Mr. John was nobody's fool. He's been with the family since Benjamin married Mama Mae long before they became wealthy.

Mae's eyes enlarged. She didn't anticipate her response as she felt that no one was aware of the truth. "Take that back and how dare you talk to me like that!"

Mary Ellen turned and peered directly in her eyes until Mae's face appeared as if it was about to shatter. She gestured with the palms of her hands. "Okay, so I made a mistake! He seemed to be a nice brother at church and he pursued me until I just couldn't take it anymore."

Mary Ellen remained focused on her sister as she listened attentively. "Okay, so what was I suppose to do—be like you and never marry? At least we're evenly yoked. We're both saved."

Mae's comment short-fused Mary Ellen. "Girl, what are you talking about? Jack is as saved as those horses are and I'm only twenty-two and I still have time to get married! I just wanted to finish school and make good of my life. Daddy worked hard and somebody needed to accomplish something!"

The carriage managed to hit a bump in the road that caused Mary Ellen's head to bump against Mae's.

"Ouch! Big head!" Mary Ellen took her hand and popped Mae's shoulder.

"You shouldn't have had your head so close to mine and you wouldn't have bumped it!" Mary Ellen laughed at Mae's shouting while she rubbed her gloved hand against her forehead. Mr. John laughed too as they could see his shoulders bouncing rhythmically.

The laughter eventually ceased as they journeyed onward toward the direction of *Beauford Place*. A spirit of calmness seemed to linger. Mae glanced at her sister and spoke gently, "I love you Little Stockings and I'm proud of you." A large grin stretched across Mary Ellen's face. The Beaufords always had high hopes for her.

She admired the surrounding land that she hadn't seen in a while. The Magnolia blossoms were lovely this time of year as they acknowledged the arrival of the long anticipated spring season. The flowers smelled redolent as Mary Ellen drew a deep breath and appreciated the fragrance.

"So tell me, has anything changed on the ranch since I've been away?"

Mae's forehead wrinkled as she searched for thoughts like a spotlight in darkness. "Let me see. Mama had one of those fancy new inventions installed where the upstairs water closet used to be. They had to destroy one of the bedrooms to widen the room and the place was a mess with all that hammering and pounding. But now it's beautiful. You'll see."

Mary Ellen tried hard to picture her description. "This I must see."

Mae rambled further, "She was going to have one sent from overseas, but a company in town sold her one and now we can all take turns washing ourselves in a steel bathtub covered with porcelain that has a wooden built-in bureau surrounding it with book shelves, and perfume, and a porcelain commode for doing you know what. And we now have a new water tank with a giant windmill that makes the water run inside instead of the workers having to fetch it."

Mary Ellen nodded. "Oh I know what you're talking about. The water tank is windmill-powered. We had one at college and I've seen them in the catalogues."

Mae pried, "No doubt you've seen a lot of things while you were gone. I'm surprised that you didn't meet any nice men. There had to at least be one nice saved man there. I thought for sure you'd be the one to write and tell us you got married."

She quipped, "I didn't go to school to get married! But I did see some pretty interesting things; I saw an electric-powered trolley that transports people and a coin-operated payphone."

Astonishment blinded Mae as Mary Ellen explained, "You put coins inside and talk to people in other places." Surprisingly Mae was unaware of this invention. She had a tendency to remain quiet in a futile attempt to appear from sounding stupid or saying something awkward.

Mae spoke sheepishly. "I forgot to mention that she added new lighting inside and outside on the grounds near the carriage house and the other quarters." She silenced herself a moment. From her expression, she appeared as if she was trying to catch the thoughts that were running around in her head. "The only other thing that I can think of is that mama had the furniture in the parlor upholstered and that's about it."

"Why? There was nothing wrong with the furniture that daddy bought." A look of concern seemed to envelope Mary Ellen.

Mae's eyes showed signs of frustration as she emitted a sigh. Hesitantly, words slowly released from her mouth. "Mama and Mr. John rode into town and came back with a rug as big as the room that didn't match the davenport and the chaise and daddy's favorite sitting chair."

It became obvious to Mary Ellen why Mae hesitated. She gave Mae's shoulder a gentle rub. "You don't have to explain. We all know how mama is—right Mr. John?"

Mr. John glanced back and gave a nod, "Sure do."

"So what else has been going on?"

"Not much. Everything's pretty much the same. Well, there is one more thing. Mama hired a new young ranchman. Mama claims that he used to help drive cattle right before they installed the railroad lines. He's a real nice fella."

Mary Ellen didn't appear to be interested in that bit of news because they've had several ranchmen. She responded nonchalantly, "That's probably why he needed work. What's his name?"

"Nathan Hickey. Everybody calls him Nate. He works really hard and that man sure loves to sing while he works," Mae emphasized as she patted her knee.

"Maybe that's how he passes the time. Sometimes I like to sing a few hymns myself. It makes me feel better, you know."

Mae snickered, "He doesn't sing hymns," and with a sly expression she added, "You'll get a chance to meet him today. I know Big Stockings sure likes to hear him sing."

Mary Ellen frowned. "Humph! Big Stockings had better like the way Robert sings! I do suppose they're still courting," she spoke emphatically while raising her brows, "and when are they going to get married?"

Mr. John snickered and Mae turned her head abruptly toward Mary Ellen while the corner of her mouth rose in a smirk, "When a rooster lays an egg! Who knows girl?"

Calmly she expressed, "She better do something before they both fall into sin."

At this point, Mr. John and Mae burst into laughter. Mary Ellen's expression clearly denoted that she didn't get it. They stopped laughing after they observed her serious countenance.

"Hold on just a minute! Do you mean to tell me that Big Stockings is sleeping around with Robert?"

Mae sucked her teeth. "I don't mean to tell you nothing and you didn't hear that from me so don't go spreading any gossip!"

"Ooh some things have changed!" Mary Ellen sunk down in her seat, nodded her head slowly from side-to-side, and spoke in a low tone of disappointment. "We were raised better than that. Daddy would surely turn over in his grave if it was possible."

Mae abruptly clasped her thick hands. "I know. He brought us all up in the church."

Mary Ellen's brows rose a second time. "What does mama have to say about this?"

Mae muttered, "I ain't saying nothing else."

Mary Ellen glanced at Mae and then looked straight ahead, as she mused concerning the turn of events. And then her head turned slowly toward Mae like a wind-up toy. She slowly uttered, "Mama doesn't know does she?"

This time Mae spoke firm with her teeth clenched, "I said I ain't saying nothing else!"

She hummed while patting her hand on her right knee. That was her way of escape when she didn't want to deal with confrontations.

"God help my sister," Mary Ellen muttered softly. Although she was the youngest sibling, she was the one that prayed the most with the exception of Mama Mae who prayed harder than all of them including the other church mothers.

The ride seemed endless as they journeyed the remainder of the way in silence. Mary Ellen appreciated seeing familiar landmarks as she continued to reverie in thought until she looked ahead and beheld a sight that was very familiar—Beauford Place! One couldn't help but take notice of Beauford Place that stood as a southern style mammoth sentinel surrounded by beautiful green country grass and the Beauford ranchland from a large distance. Its picturesque view appeared to be celestial as large pillow-like clouds appeared to rest around its upper portion.

Her reverie of the morning events had come to a close as she prepared herself to face the crowd awaiting her downstairs.

Chapter Two

Mary Ellen's heart pounded as she gracefully emerged down the staircase while her lovely dress swept over each step as the noise from the crinoline annoyed her. She tried to anticipate what to expect from all the opulence while her onlookers displayed expressions of admiration. Many eyes were focused on her especially from the men, as she became the focal point for the remainder of the evening. She had changed into a lovely pastel pink long-flowing dress with pink floral petals around her neckline. Her black crinkly thick locks of hair hung loosely from her shoulders and midway down her back. She looked radiant and beautiful.

Uncle Addison photographed her well until her pupils nearly dilated. Mama Mae insisted that he photograph her outside the mansion as well. She stood posed as she held her breath in the tightly fastened corset while he snapped the camera. She looked up and noticed that Nathan had been watching the entire time as well as some of the brethren from church and men from neighboring homes.

Everyone including the workers helped themselves to enormous helpings of southern fried chicken, barbecued pork, and steak along with fixings that consisted of macaroni and cheese, cornbread, collard, and kale greens cooked with fatback, kettle-cooked sauce beans with bacon, triple layered cakes, and more. The Beaufords treated Nathan and the other workers as if they were all kindred.

One of the women from the church choir belted out a song that she had written for the occasion. Mary Ellen's eyes watered. She had missed the foot stomping down home church services. The church services that she attended during college were a little too conservative for her. She heard melodic sounds of someone playing skillfully on a guitar. She glanced around and was surprised to see Nathan strumming a guitar and then something else drew her attention. It was Marva serving Robert dessert and collecting his plate as if they were married. Mary Ellen silently expressed her disapproval of their display by releasing a sigh of frustration.

Nevertheless, she decided not to allow this to ruin her triumphant moment and time of jubilee.

It was good for her to see Mama Mae happily bustling about acknowledging and thanking everyone for their participation. The last time she saw Mama Mae was at her father's funeral. She had hoped that her mother would be happy again as many prayers had proceeded from her innermost being.

Mary Ellen slipped away for a brief moment, walked inside to the parlor, and stared at the large portrait of her father dressed in one of his favorite going-to-town suits. He was a handsome man with a black moustache that turned up at the ends. His hairline was grayed. His countenance displayed the serious look that he often had. Mary Ellen was the only sibling that inherited the serious side of her father. Mama Mae had a small brass plate affixed to the lower part of the frame, which read: *Benjamin Beauford, Beloved Husband, Father, and Inventor.* Those were the very words inscribed on his tombstone at the burial ground on their ranch. She carefully ran her fingers across the brass plate, smiled, and said, "Thank you daddy. I made it by the grace of God and your hard work and diligence."

The sound of Marva and Robert sneaking inside the mansion interrupted her reverie. Marva's eyes enlarged and Robert tried to be circumspect while Mary Ellen looked upon them with firmness, as she had been precocious since childhood. "Does mama know?"

"We were uh—just coming inside to get away from the crowd for a bit. There's just too many people out there for me so Robert thought it would be best if we stepped inside for a little bit."

Mary Ellen's face displayed her disappointment and they realized that she knew. "When are you two going to set a wedding date? I thought you'd be married long before I finished school."

Marva smiled and let out a brief nervous laugh. Robert stopped trying to fake a smile because he realized that their little secret had been exposed. Marva tried to shift the burden to Robert.

"You see Robert here," she patted his shoulder while her eyes remained focused on Mary Ellen, "is trying to get his self together first because he's been helping his folks and after that we're going to get married." Marva glanced at Robert as she anticipated him to nod or do something to corroborate her story. Robert stood motionless as he studied Mary Ellen.

Mary Ellen never trusted him from the time he approached Marva at the general store and was invited to attend church services with her. He attended the services as long as Marva insisted. Nonetheless, his attention seemed to be always focused on other women; Mary Ellen in particular who would always give him a contemptuous sneer as if to say, *if you don't get out of my face, I'll tell my sister.*

Finally, Mary Ellen spoke, "However you choose to live your lives is between you and the Lord. But don't go doing your business in daddy's house! You know he would never have allowed it and neither will mama should she find out."

Mary Ellen left them where they stood and exited the mansion as quietly as she could amid the sound of her crinoline. As the evening drew to a close, many of the guests congratulated and hugged Mary Ellen again before their departure. She decided to sit on the wooden swing attached to the front verandah. She watched Mama Mae standing near the roadside talking with some of the relatives who were leaving. She would occasionally laugh because her family talked very loud and Mama Mae could be hilarious at times. She had a tendency to pronounce words in her own unique way. It was a vain attempt to correct her grammar because whenever anyone tried to cross that boundary it was done amiss. Mama Mae would always explain that she didn't have much schooling when she was a small girl growing up in the Deep South.

She met Benjamin while working as a chambermaid. They married and he had aspirations to further their livelihood. Therefore, they moved to Tradassa Town to start fresh so that he could try out some inventions that he used to jot down on notes.

Mary Ellen heard a sound and turned to see who was opening the screened door. "It's just me Little Stockings." Mae decided to join her on the front verandah. Mary Ellen extended her arms to block her. "Girl don't sit on this swing with me! It might break from the rafters."

Mae laughed. "Hush child. I was fixing to sit here in this chair where daddy used to sit." Mary Ellen rocked lightly as she began to unwind from all the excitement. A moment later, she stopped rocking. Small wrinkles shot across her forehead as she looked at Mae.

"So tell me," she spoke in a whisper, "why didn't you say that the new ranchman was a colored man?"

Mae shrugged her shoulders. "Must've slipped my mind. I must've figured you knew somehow. He's a good sight to look at ain't he?"

Mary Ellen smiled although she didn't want to. She leaned toward Mae and spoke in a low tone, "Now I'm going to tell you to hush and leave it alone. Just leave it alone girl. The Beauford women have made enough mistakes when it comes to choosing the right man for a husband. The only one that did good was mama and I aim to go in her direction!"

Mae nodded in agreement, as she patted her full belly. "But—."

Mary Ellen clenched her teeth and quipped, "But nothing! I said leave it alone!"

Mae was good at changing the subject. "You seen Big Stockings?"

Mary Ellen crooked her mouth. "Yeah, I've seen Big Stockings and big trouble."

Mae murmured and rocked her right foot, "Lordy, Lordy, um-um-um. Lord help us all. Now you see why I said that I wasn't saying nothing."

Mary Ellen seemed dismayed. "A lot has changed since daddy died. I remember when he used to have us all praying together as a family and now it seems like that special element is missing."

Mae patted herself on the knee and spoke, "Yeah daddy was the prayer warrior of this family. Now the mantle's been handed down to mama."

Mary Ellen concluded, "Poor mama. She's got her hands full. It seemed like when we had less we were closer to God somehow."

Mae raised her head, "It does. Doesn't it?"

Mary Ellen nodded in agreement.

A few minutes later, she looked up and saw Nathan approaching the front verandah. They could hear him singing. He poised himself against one of the thick wooden posts. He still had on his black cowboy hat and leather boots and his face was clean-shaven. "Evening ladies."

Both women responded, "Evening."

Mae's grin appeared somewhat sinister. Mary Ellen gave a normal smile.

Mae continued to grin and Nathan smiled as usual—but not at Mae. His attention was focused on Mary Ellen. He finally spoke. "Did you enjoy your party?"

Mary Ellen seemed somewhat surprised. "Yes I did. It was very nice and especially your guitar music."

He smiled again. "I'm glad you liked it. It was the least I could do."

Mae continued to grin as she studied their reactions. Mama Mae approached and patted Nathan's shoulder. "You did real good today helping out with everything. I really appreciate that."

He gave a generous smile. "Thanks ma'am."

Mama Mae looked at Mary Ellen. "You know I forgot to introduce you to Little Stockings. I've been so busy and all."

Mary Ellen interrupted with a look of embarrassment, "Mama we've already been introduced. I was just telling Nathan that I enjoyed his guitar playing at the party."

Mama Mae was still full of excitement as she vociferated, "Oh yeah. We enjoyed it!" She gave a gentle pat to Nathan's shoulder as he chuckled.

Mary Ellen was tired from the long day and was feeling drowsy as she slowly rose to her feet. While she hugged and kissed her mother, her eyes met with Nathan's as if they were peering through one another's pupils. She immediately withdrew herself. "Mama, I must get some rest. Thanks for everything. Good night everybody."

Mama Mae whispered in her ear, "You know your father would be proud."

Everyone went their way to retire for the evening. Nathan proceeded to the carriage house. Benjamin and Mama Mae ensured that their workers lived comfortably on the property. They did this because when they used to perform hard labor long before Benjamin's success, no one saw to their comfort. Besides, this kept the workers happy.

Mary Ellen knelt to pray before she climbed into bed. She prayed for everyone in her family for God to draw them near to Him as tears flowed down her cheeks. She prayed especially hard for Marva and Robert.

She climbed into bed and somehow couldn't fall asleep right away although she found herself both weary and restless from the turn of events. The stars were brightly lit in the sky as if they were sparkling diamonds placed there one-by-one. Her window was open as a fresh night zephyr cooled the room. She could hear sounds of the creatures. Her mind still seemed to race from all the traveling, arriving at the station in the morning along with the evening festivities, and seeing old and new faces. She had finally accomplished her goal. Her dream had been realized albeit she longed for her father's presence on the ranch. Being home just didn't feel the same.

A spirit of loneliness seemed to taunt her. Still feeling restless, Mary Ellen climbed out of bed as if something beckoned to her. She turned on a small lamp, removed a long chiffon robe, and put it on. Mary Ellen unlocked the double-doors and stepped onto the verandah, looked up at the stars, and drew a deep breath. She uttered, "Thank You Lord for seeing me through these years and getting me home safely."

She pivoted, returned inside, locked the doors, and stood in front of her window. She could see fireflies flying about as if they were taking turns twinkling. A closed-mouth smiled emerged. Mary Ellen positioned herself comfortably on the floor while resting her head on the windowsill and stared into the night until she drifted off to a deep slumber.

Chapter Three

Somehow, Nathan's voice seemed to overshadow the songbirds at the crack of dawn. It sounded as if the birds chirped along with his singing. Mary Ellen had slept on the floor throughout the night and was awakened by his crooning. She slowly lifted herself up to peek out of the window. It was bright and early—a little too early. He seemed to happily attend to his chores. He didn't realize that she was watching him. It was then that she felt comfortable with her family's choice for hiring him.

Feeling that she could no longer withstand being inside, she prepared herself so that she could go outside and enjoy the start of the lovely morning. Her pastel purple dress and matching spool-heeled shoes made her look ladylike. As she was seated at her fold-up vanity, she realized that her hair was mussed and didn't want to be seen like that. It resembled long large wads of dark crinkly cotton. She combed through it and finally plaited it in one long braid that hung down her back with a matching ribbon on the bottom. It resembled a long broided black rope. She felt somewhat childish, yet presentable.

Mary Ellen was elated when she discovered that the family hadn't awakened yet. She slowly crept downstairs and decided to take advantage of the peace and quiet. She walked into her father's former study, snatched a fountain pen and some paper from a stand positioned next to a typewriter, and went outside to the front verandah. It had always been her favorite place.

Mary Ellen majored in classical literature. She took time to write a poem and then carefully scanned it with her eyes for completion. Afterwards, she rested her eyes and slowly rocked on the wooden swing until a noise frightened her. Her eyes flung open and she saw Nathan standing on the steps. "Morning Miss. Didn't mean to frighten you."

Feeling somewhat embarrassed, she composed herself by straightening her seated posture. "Good morning. You did frighten me a little." She could no longer restrain her laughter and he chuckled.

Her eyes roamed like a searchlight as she carefully studied his face including the distinctive slight cleft in his chin. "I had just finished writing a poem and decided to relax."

His eyes were warm and friendly. His brown lips were somewhat medium – not quite full. His dark brows weren't heavy either. He stood about six foot two and was strong in body and mind.

"Your sisters told me that you majored in classical literature. That's interesting because I'm not accustomed to being around a lady like you."

Smiling gingerly, she felt glad to be appreciated. He carefully studied her as if he was apprehensive and chose to prevent himself from blurting something offensive. She realized that he wasn't at all the bashful type—just careful. It became obvious to her that although he was young like her that he was a man of worldly wisdom and without a doubt experienced in areas that she hadn't dared to venture in. She found him somewhat intriguing but not enough for her to become inquisitive at the moment. Nonetheless, it didn't stop his inquisitiveness.

"Do you mind if I ask you a question?"

Mary Ellen's fear haunted her and her heart pounded as she hesitated. "Not at all."

"Why do they call you *Little Stockings*?"

They both laughed heartily. She tried to respond while laughing.

"It all started with daddy. It's like this; my sister Marva is the medium built one and I have the smallest frame and Big Mae's named after mama. They call her that because she's sort of corpulent." She laughed despite her embarrassment.

He chuckled again as his eyes squinted. "That's understandable. What's your real name?"

She cleared her throat and poised herself again. "Mary Ellen."

This time he didn't smile. "That's a nice name. Mary Ellen I'd like to hear your poem."

Her lashes fluttered somewhat nervously. "I—I really don't think that it's the type of poem that you would be interested in hearing. It's uh—."

He emerged from the steps, relaxed in her father's former chair, and placed his hat on the ledge. "Well—are you going to read it or not?"

He reminded her of her father for a brief moment. She was stunned by his firmness and calm demeanor. There was something about him that made her feel at ease during that moment. She slowly began to recite the poem as he listened attentively.

"It's titled *A Time for Celebration!*
Tis' a time of celebration, blessing, and honor,
To a notable lady that became God's scholar.
Dr. Mary Ellen Beauford is my true name,
Albeit I did it not for fortune nor fame.
I've labored especially hard for my finals this year,
While encouraging other scholars to be of good cheer.
I also proclaimed the teachings of Christ,
To those who received it whether naughty or nice.
I try to give God my very best,
Because of Him, I am truly blessed.
The Lord has been my Comforter throughout joy and sorrow,
And He will still be there for me on the morrow.
Jesus carried me upon heavenly wings during my plight,
As He listened to my prayers throughout day and night.
My heart need not worry nor fear any trouble,
Because Jesus loves me and will be there on the double.
My loved ones are blessed throughout this Beauford land,
Including my father as he sleeps in the palm of His hand.
My purpose is to stand on the promises of God,
While arrayed in battle armor with my feet tightly shod.
Not only do I declare God's Holy Word,

I'm blessed with a voice to sing as God's songbird.
May the Lord continue to keep me as I am celebrated,
For accomplishing a dream that I have long awaited."

Her eyes slowly met his as she anticipated his reaction toward her recital. His expression was sincere. "That was really nice. I have to admit that I enjoyed it."

They became quiet for a moment as they peered into one another's eyes until she caught her breath and stood. While enveloped in fear again, she nervously managed to speak while her eyes remained fixated on his. "I'd—I'd better go back inside. I haven't eaten breakfast yet and I don't want to detain you from your chores. I'm sure that you have better things to do than listen to my poetry."

He stood and placed his cowboy hat back on his head and nodded. "Thank you for your time Mary Ellen." He proceeded down the steps and then turned around as if he had forgotten something. Mary Ellen stood motionless as if she was petrified while uneasiness crept upon her because she didn't know what to expect.

"I have a horse that I tamed that I'd like to give you for a graduation present."

She was immediately loosed from her fear as her eyes seemed to light up and she resumed her seated position.

"Really—what's its name?"

"Rain."

Her forehead wrinkled as she questioned, "Rein?"

He laughed and explained. "Like Rain that falls from the sky."

Her countenance transitioned to laughter. "Oh—I thought you meant rein like pertaining to a horse." They grimaced. "Rain is a nice name."

He turned slightly and stared in the direction of the corral while a gleam of sunlight flashed on his belt buckle that caused her eyes to water as she squinted. She held her hand upward to block the vivid sunbeam that caused his belt buckle to coruscate. "Your belt buckle is blinding me."

He swiftly shifted his position on the steps. "My apologies Miss. This buckle does attract a great deal of sunlight. I used to use it to let other riders—," shamefacedly he lowered his head and raised it again, "know where I was."

Mary Ellen didn't notice his hesitation as she batted her watery lashes and blotted them with her finger. He removed his neckerchief and blotted her eyes.

"Thank you. What does NJH stand for?"

He glanced downward at his buckle. "Nathan Jonah Hickey—Nathan was my father's name."

Subconsciously he curled up his lips in disgust in anticipation of what he was about to say. "And my mother wanted me to have a name from the Bible so she named me Jonah."

She propped her elbow on the arm of the swing and leaned the side of her face against her fist. Inquisitively she questioned, "Why did you frown just now?"

"What do mean?"

She peered into his eyes. "You frowned when you were mentioning the name Jonah. Do you dislike that name?" Her brows rose.

He tipped his hat frustratingly then proceeded down the steps that consisted of only two and strutted swiftly toward the corral. She stood on the steps and watched him until he entered the stables. Guilt permeated her heart as the wind of frustration emitted from her being. She didn't know whether she offended him although curiosity piqued her attention. She wanted to pursue to learn what upset him, then her heart filled with pride at that moment, and therefore her legs wouldn't budge.

Within minutes, her countenance lit up as a smile unzipped its way from her lips; for out of the stables emerged the most beautiful black mare that her eyes have ever beheld. He walked alongside it and brushed its fine black mane.

"Rain!" she uttered softly. Her smile resumed and she waved. Pride had slipped away from her. He beckoned for her presence. She grabbed the sides of her dress and bolted toward the stables. Her long braid flung around as a kite soaring through the windy sky.

Rain was more beautiful close up than in distance. Mary Ellen was elated as she shouted, "This is Rain!"

Nathan grinned while he brushed the noble creature. "How'd you know?"

While her heart beat vehemently from running she responded, "I don't know. I just knew."

He laughed, "You're short-winded. Do you feel up to riding her?"

She sucked wind, "Why do you think I ran all the way over here?"

He had hoped that it was to see him but he knew better. He saddled Rain and before he could assist her on the mare, she quickly mounted and rode away. He ran inside the stables, brought out his horse, quickly mounted, and pursued the woman of his dreams. He caught up with her as the wind seemed to carry them as if they were one in God and nature. Neither of them realized that there were two sets of highly inquisitive watchful eyes peering at them albeit they had nothing to hide. They were enjoying a nice breezy ride on the property.

She finally slowed Rain down and then came to a halt. "Whoa!" Nearly out of breath, she looked at Nathan who had stopped alongside her.

"You know something, I'm hungry. I didn't have breakfast."

He retrieved a small pouch that was tied to his belt loop and extended it to her. Not knowing what to expect she peered inside. A smile transformed her face as she reached for a piece of beef jerky. She glanced at him. "Thanks I needed this. I think between running through the field and riding that I needed something to eat."

She basked in the moment as if she dined on a juicy T-bone steak. Nathan decided to partake of their convenient breakfast as he chewed a couple of pieces.

"I better get you back so that I can finish my chores. Besides, I don't want to get in any trouble with Mama Mae. She's been real kind to me."

"You needn't worry about that. Mama seems to like you." He didn't respond as they journeyed toward the stables at a slow pace. He started singing. That was the defining moment that led her to realize why Marva admired his crooning. She too had been awestruck! He sang beautifully. Moreover, Mae was right—he didn't sing hymnals!

Mary Ellen would occasionally steal glances at him. "You have a nice voice. That's a gift from God you know. You shouldn't waste it singing useless songs."

"What kind of songs do you think I should sing?" He awaited her reply with an intent countenance that caused her to feel slightly intimidated. Immediately, she wished that somehow she could retract her latter statement.

He conceded. "I guess I don't deserve an answer." An aura of silence overshadowed them until they reached the stables. He assisted her off Rain and she gave a curt, "Thank you," and he gently lifted his hat in a gentleman-like manner. She proceeded in the direction of the mansion. His eyes remained fixated on her the entire time as she stepped on the front verandah, grabbed her poem and pen, and then disappeared from his view.

Chapter Four

Seated around the large mahogany rectangular shaped table were Mama Mae, Mae, Jack, Marva, and Mary Ellen. Mama Mae sat in her usual place in a larger chair at one end of the table. Another larger empty chair was positioned in authority at the other end of the table. It was carved differently from the others albeit it matched the table. No one had occupied it since Benjamin expired. Mary Ellen was away at college the day Mama Mae entered the study and found him slumped over on his desk. She left everything as it was.

Immediately after the blessing of their food, they were interrupted by a knock at the front door. Mr. John answered and escorted Robert into the dining area to join the others. Robert quickly plopped himself in the ornate large empty chair as if there were no other empty chairs available. He was unashamed to depict his non-gentleman like qualities.

Mary Ellen's eyes enlarged as she peered at him in disbelief. She glanced at the others around the table to discern their expressions. All remained silent. Mae's eyes met with Mary Ellen's that displayed their nondescript way of expressing disapproval with this arrangement.

Mary Ellen's countenance became far too obvious to Mae who realized that she had better stop her anticipated reaction. Mae gave a slight nod of her head sideways in a futile attempt to signal Mary Ellen who clearly disregarded it.

Pap! Mary Ellen popped her napkin on the table while everyone's eyes widened with the exception of Robert's. Mama Mae quickly inquired, "Baby what's the matter? Were you trying to kill a fly or something?" Everyone else knew what happened that brought on her bellicose mood.

"No mama. I just don't think that it's right for Robert to parade in here and sit in daddy's chair!"

Marva pleaded, "Little Stockings leave it alone. Just leave it alone. It'll be alright. You'll see."

Mary Ellen blurted, "I'm tired of being called Little Stockings! And that's not all," Mae, Marva, and Robert's faces were shrouded in fear in anticipation of what she was about to say, "He didn't even wash his hands before he came in here and nobody invited him for breakfast!"

Mama Mae beckoned everyone to calm down with her hands as if conducting a choir and then spoke emphatically, "The Bible says it ain't no sin to eat with unwashed hands because unwashed hands ain't what defiles a man. It's what comes out of a man that defiles him. Although I prefer that everyone wash their hands in the Beauford household," she placed her hand across her bosom, "I can't rightly judge nobody neither. The good Lord blessed us Beaufords and we've always shared—even when we didn't have much to share!"

Everyone around the table agreed by saying, "Amen," with the exception of Mary Ellen who abruptly excused herself from the table then stood and faced everyone.

"The Bible also says, for nothing is secret, that shall not be made manifest," her eyes filled with tears and she scurried upstairs to her room.

Mama Mae was astounded because she didn't understand her behavior. When they passed the food around, Mama Mae sighed as wrinkles appeared on her forehead, "I don't know what's bothering Little Stockings. She seemed very happy until Robert walked in the room. I sure hope that having a degree don't make her think she's better than everybody."

Everyone purposely ignored her comment by focusing on eating because they knew that her education had nothing to do with it. It was their church upbringing.

Mary Ellen flung herself across her bed and wept until she heard the sound of Nathan busily working and singing a familiar song. It was an old hymnal that her father used to sing. She realized that Nathan changed his song and being closed up in her bedroom wasn't doing her any good notwithstanding the fact that she felt childish. She spruced herself up and loosened her hair to allow her locks to flow freely. She snatched her tiny Bible on her way out of the bedroom and gracefully descended each stair as if her legs were fingers gently stroking a finely tuned piano. When she reached the stoop, she glanced toward the direction of the dining room where she could hear voices and silverware tingling against the dishes and then proceeded to the front verandah.

Mary Ellen desperately wanted to get her mind off negativity. One thing that she enjoyed doing since she was a small girl was to swing from the grand live oak tree. She had always found peace swinging while staring at the beautiful cerulean sky and reading Scriptures. She had ensured that her father maintained the swing. Now Mr. John maintains it for her.

Mary Ellen closed her eyes for a while as she glided through the air on the swing. She clutched the ropes taut and leaned back as far as she could while her loose locks of hair appeared to dance in the wind.

Later that afternoon, the Beauford women sat around on the front verandah as they sipped cold tea and reminisced of old times. Mary Ellen gently rocked on the swing. Marva displayed a suspicious countenance, as she felt guilt-hearted toward God and Mary Ellen. Mae was being her sly inquisitive self while Mama Mae was completely unaware as to what the situation entailed although she sensed that something was in the mix. Jack was lazily napping on the hammock underneath a shade tree in the back. Nathan had finished his chores and went fishing at the Beauford Brook. Miss Beatrice, the cook was peeling and slicing peaches in the kitchen. Miss Edna the housekeeper was busy tidying the rooms. Moreover, Mr. Pope had just finished tending to the cattle.

"Did you enjoy yourself this morning?" The women glared at Mae with questionable expressions with the exception of Mary Ellen who spoke up. "She's speaking to me." She positioned herself upright on the swing. "Yes, I did enjoy myself this morning. Is there anything else you'd like to know?" Mae nodded responsively to '*no.*'

This time Marva spoke up. "Did I miss something?"

A puzzled expression overshadowed Mama Mae as she underscored Marva's inquiry. "I was wondering the same thing. It's sure been a strange day. Everybody's been behavin' sort of strange. I can't rightly place what's going on. But I know something's in the kettle."

Mary Ellen cleared her throat and then took a sip of lemonade. "If it's anyone's concern, I took a sunrise ride on the ranch with Nathan on separate horses. He gave me the most beautiful mare that I've ever seen named Rain as a graduation present."

Marva's eyes lit up while Mama Mae smiled. Marva's expression clearly underscored her disapproval with Mama Mae's reaction. Therefore, she spoke candidly, "And you showed out this morning at breakfast because of me and Robert and you went out gallivanting around with Nate!" Everyone knew that Robert was notorious for cajoling Marva as well as other women.

"Hush up!" Mama Mae shouted. "She didn't do no wrong. Besides, Nate's a fine young man. Your father wouldn't have hired him if he wasn't. He reminds me of your father when he was young." Mary Ellen was taken aback at her mother's reaction.

"That's the problem! She's always been daddy's girl. Daddy was always disappointed in me."

Mama Mae stood with one hand on her hip and with the other; she pointed her finger at Marva. "Don't you dare take that out on Little Stockings! Before your father passed away he told me that you *was* sleeping around with Robert and that he's heard stories of Robert seeing other women while he's been seeing you." Marva's eyes displayed a slight shock and disappointment. Mae realized that she had opened a can of worms. It didn't take Mary Ellen long to figure out that Mae and Jack had been watching her ride with Nathan.

Mama Mae continued while the others were recovering from their expressions of disbelief at their mother's outburst. "For all you know, he could've gave you the nasty woman's disease. What *was* you thinking about? And then you got the nerve to brush the crumbs off your face and sit up in church and sing in the choir as if God don't see you. It don't work like that baby!"

Mary Ellen lowered her head in frustration while her hands covered her face. "Mama what happened while I was away? Our family used to live godly and now it seems like since daddy died, it's just not the same. He was the pillar of this family and when you knock a pillar down from a foundation we all know what you get."

Mae interjected, "Yeah it's like when Samson pushed the pillars out."

Mama Mae added, "And the foundation and everything fell upon the Philistines."

Mary Ellen wiped her eyes. "I can't wait to be at church tomorrow. I really need to be there." They agreed in unison. Feeling empathetic, she got up and hugged Marva and then they all joined in a group hug. Marva cried on her sister's shoulder, "I'm," sniff, "going to have a hearty talk with Robert and he's going to have to make a decision 'cause I can't keep going on like this."

Mary Ellen kissed her sister's forehead. "I'm sorry for the way I behaved at breakfast." Tears flowed down her cheeks while she concluded firmly, "And for the record ladies, there is nothing going on betwixt Nathan and I," as she placed her hand on her bosom. "There is no romantic interest whatsoever."

Mae chimed, "Now hold on a minute. There may be no romantic interest on your part but there's some on his part. I know what I'm talking about 'cause I can tell by the way his eyes google when he looks at you."

A chuckle had finally released from Marva and her eyes lit up. "I know girl 'cause he sure doesn't look at anybody else the way he looks at her. And you know his singing has increased since Little Stockings came home."

Mama Mae laughed heartily, "Ooh child!"

Mae added more commentary, "And he never used to come to the front verandah and talk."

Mary Ellen smirked. "I don't care what he never used to do and I don't care what you all say, I'm not going to marry a ranchman! I want a man that's refined and saved of course."

Mama Mae's laughter roared. "Refined and saved huh! The good Lord works in mysterious ways. When I met your father, he wasn't refined and saved. God eventually saved him just like he saved me."

She kissed her mother's cheek. "Mama please stop putting wood in the fire. Leave it alone."

Just when the women regained their composure, Nathan approached from the side of the mansion with a cart that contained a large metal scrub bucket brimming with catfish. "Afternoon ladies." He smiled as usual.

"What you got there son?" Mama Mae eyed the fish. "I hope you plan to share 'cause I loves me some fried catfish." She patted her belly and a smile widened on Nathan's face as he chuckled.

And of course Big Mae added, "Me too."

Mama Mae's eyes lit up as she stood and peered into the container. "Look at the size of that one!" One of the catfish looked as if it weighed approximately forty pounds. He exclaimed, "Took me a while to catch that one. He got away from me a few times."

The others peered into the container and exclaimed, "Wow!"

"Why don't you give that catfish to Mr. John so he can clean it and tell him to have Miss Beatrice fry some of it for supper."

"Mama, I think she'll only need to cook the one fish 'cause that's enough to feed all of us," Mae spoke in astonishment.

Mama Mae declared, "She knows what to do. Now don't just stand there grinning. Go and get yourself cleaned up and join us for supper."

"Yes ma'am." Nathan looked surprised because he had never joined the family for supper. He had eaten outdoors with Benjamin occasionally during lunch when they would have hearty man-to-man discussions. Benjamin treated him like a son albeit he didn't treat Jack and Robert that way. Jack and Robert were well aware as to the reason why he didn't much care for them.

Mary Ellen's eyes enlarged, "Mama he might have other plans and we shouldn't take his catfish. He was probably planning on sharing it with Miss Edna and Mr. Pope."

Nathan spoke up. "No ma'am I hadn't planned on sharing with the others. I thought you'd all like to have this fish for supper. After all, I caught them from your brook."

Mama Mae smiled, "Son, you know you're welcome to fish from the brook anytime you please and if you want to keep the fish for yourself, you're welcome to do so. I just happen to love catfish."

His attention was focused primarily on Mary Ellen. "I'll take this fish around to Mr. John and I'll see you ladies at suppertime." He gently gestured by slightly lifting his hat and then departed.

Jack, Mae, Mama Mae, and Nathan of course were seated around the rectangular-shaped table on one side from left to right. On the opposite side from left to right sat Mary Ellen, Robert, Marva, and Mr. John, which Mama Mae had asked to join them at the spur of the moment. Mary Ellen and Nathan were seated directly across one another, which made Mary Ellen a bit uncomfortable. Benjamin's former favorite chair and the one that Mama Mae usually sat in at the opposite end of the table remained empty.

Miss Beatrice entered the room wearing a large long white apron over her dress and a matching white cotton mobcap with ruffles that completely covered her hair. She's been with the family a long time as well as the other workers with the exception of Nathan. Miss Edna assisted her in bringing the platters of food.

Miss Edna is a little younger than Miss Beatrice and Mama Mae. She wore her hair pulled back in a bun along with her uniform that consisted of an ankle-length long-sleeved black dress with a white apron and a white mobcap.

Mr. Pope is older than Nathan and a well-seasoned rancher. The workers usually dined at a table located in the kitchen, sometimes outdoors, and sometimes in their living quarters that consisted of neatly furnished smaller built housing units on the property. All of the workers attend the same church as the Beauford family—all except Nathan.

Miss Edna and Miss Beatrice served from the left a hearty meal that consisted of southern fried catfish, butter beans, asparagus, and mouth-watering cornbread with butter oozing down the sides.

Miss Beatrice placed one of her freshly baked peach cobblers on the table and everyone smiled. The aroma of cinnamon and fresh vanilla tantalized their senses as they anticipated finishing their main course.

Mae commented, "Miss Beatrice, your peach cobblers are so good, makes me want to pat my foot when I eat it!" Miss Beatrice laughed sheepishly as she exited the room while the others laughed. Miss Edna followed her out. Marva added, "You sure 'nough told the truth there. Miss Beatrice must put her foot in her cobblers 'cause they taste so good!"

Everyone laughed again. Nathan laughed to the point that his eyes welled with tears. Mary Ellen glanced at Nathan, "Will you two please stop it! Nathan's over here laughing so hard that he's about to cry."

As the platters were being passed around, Mary Ellen couldn't help but notice that Nathan looked unmistakably handsome. His dark face was smooth and clean-shaven as the slight cleft in his chin prominently accentuated his features. His mild deep brown eyes appeared comforting and soothing. She could smell his after-shave and cologne although the scent of the cobbler filled the room. She studied his hands and realized that it was the first time that she had noticed them without the black leather gloves. His hands were rough in the palms and the upper portions were somewhat smooth—perhaps from being protected with the gloves. She then realized that it was the first time she had paid close attention to him without his black cowboy hat.

His hair is a deep brown color that was neatly cut approximately less than a quarter of an inch. It was parted on the left side and had a slight crinkly wave pattern that encircled the crown of his head and lay down neatly as if it had been scarf-tied at night. She figured that he probably tied it around his head underneath his hat to alleviate sweat from pouring down his face while he's working. His neatly pressed white cotton western shirt helped to secure his black cross-over style western necktie in place. He wore a black weskit. She didn't want to appear obvious that she had been studying him, so she would snatch glances.

The clattering of dishes finally ceased as they prepared to bless their meal. They usually took turns after Benjamin's departure. Mama Mae eyed Nathan. "Nate, why don't you bless the food. You haven't had a turn."

He spoke hesitantly, "Ma'am I'm not in any position to pray."

Mary Ellen drew a deep breath and hoped that her mother would select someone else to do the honor. But no, Mama Mae had to pry and Mae was hoping that she would dig deep into Nathan's personal affairs since her life seemed to lack any real interest. Mr. John simply wanted this to end so that he could delve into the delicacies. Robert and Jack were glad that she didn't select them. Marva desired to pray to get it over and done with. Nevertheless, she knew better than to interfere.

"What do you mean son? Anybody can pray."

Mary Ellen could see that he felt uncomfortable and therefore chose to intervene. She looked deep into his eyes and spoke, "Mama, perhaps he doesn't know how to pray. I'll bless the food this time and I promise to teach Nathan how to pray another time." She patted his hand gently to comfort him and then asked everyone to bow their heads in reverence to God and proceeded to pray.

Afterwards, everyone raised their heads and began eating. Nathan looked at Mary Ellen and thanked her as he winced, gave a slight nod, and smiled with his lips closed. They both felt relieved. Miss Edna returned and poured cold tea into their fancy crystal goblets, which they normally only used for Sunday dinners. Nevertheless, Mama Mae wanted their best crystal and china used today. No one could understand why. Nathan held his goblet toward Mary Ellen to toast hers. She was surprised and so were the others as they stared when their goblets made a tingling sound. Mae glanced at Jack to see whether he would do her that way. He continued to devour his food and never paid much attention to her. Marva looked at Robert and noticed that he had practically consumed his tea.

It was time to pass the cobbler as the others had heaped it on their dessert plates. Mary Ellen had scooped a little on hers. She looked up at Nathan. "Would you care for some cobbler?" He handed her his dessert plate. She didn't anticipate him doing that. She scooped some on his plate. "Would you like more or is this enough?"

He responded politely, "A little more would be fine."

She carefully scooped more and as she positioned the cobbler dish in a more suitable spot on the table, she couldn't help but feel that all eyes were upon her and Nathan. She glanced toward their direction and her instincts were correct. Mae had especially leaned over for the occasion to catch a good view.

Nathan depicted the qualities of a true gentleman albeit she could tell that he had been through a lot to be a year younger. He ate well and Mary Ellen realized that he thoroughly enjoyed the supper. He blotted his mouth with his napkin.

Mae's voice thundered across the table at Nathan. "That cobbler was good like I said—wasn't it?"

He gave a nod then answered, "It was delicious. It reminded me of my mother's."

A sinister look appeared on Mae's face. "When's the last time you seen your mother?"

He hesitated briefly and then responded, "At her funeral." Silence swept through the room along with a spirit of empathy. Mae realized that she had put her foot in her mouth this time.

Mary Ellen felt a jolt shoot through her body. She knew that something was there that he never mentioned. The only one that he shared anything confidential to was Benjamin because he knew that their father would conceal the matter, as he was trustworthy. For the first time Mary Ellen peered into his eyes and could see that he had been hurt. There lie within him wounds that needed to be healed. She felt as if she wanted to actually befriend him for the first time as opposed to shunning him. She didn't know if she could help tear down the wall that he had built. And whether she possessed the strength and courage to help him.

Miss Edna returned with a pot of coffee and Miss Beatrice carried a tray of cups with matching saucers. Miss Edna gently placed a saucer and cup at everyone's setting and poured coffee while Miss Beatrice held the tray. Afterwards, they exited the room and returned with one carrying a pitcher of cream and the other carrying a sugar bowl.

Mary Ellen gave Nathan a genuine tender smile for the first time. She held the sugar bowl. "Would you like some sugar?"

His eyes lit up as he returned the smile albeit he knew that she meant actual sugar. "Sure." He slid his coffee over as she scooped some in. "Would you like more?"

He responded, "That's enough" as he didn't care for his coffee to be sweet.

"Cream?" She raised her brows at him in anticipation of his reply.

"Please, just a little."

He slid his coffee toward his direction and stirred it while his eyes were fixated upon hers. Mary Ellen's instincts told her that everyone was peering at them and once again, she was correct. She decided to ignore their inquisitiveness—especially Mae's.

They sipped their coffee quietly and gazed at one another until he finally broke the silence. "How'd you like Rain?"

"I love her."

"When do you plan to ride her again?"

She placed her china cup on the saucer and blotted her lips. "I'd like to ride her tomorrow. But I'll be at church. And after that we usually have Sunday supper."

"I know." Mary Ellen forgot that Nathan had been on the ranch for some time while she was away at college. Before she realized, she blurted, "Do you plan to have supper with us again tomorrow?" She couldn't believe that she asked him that. Nevertheless, it was too late to retract her question.

He placed his china cup down on its saucer then peered into her deep brown eyes. "Would you like me to?"

This time Mae wasn't the only one that leaned over to be nosey. Everyone leaned to hear her reply.

Nervously, she didn't quite know what to say as she stammered over her words, "I—uh well—." Before she could finish he interrupted, "It's okay. I understand."

She insisted on trying to come up with something to say and failed. "Well—it's—uh—."

He gestured with his hand. "You don't need to explain. I understand."

He gently patted her hand and spoke slowly while staring into her eyes, "When the time is right and you feel comfortable, you'll invite me."

Her lashes fluttered as she stared at him. She didn't know what came over her. Suddenly Mary Ellen found herself in a position that she never thought would happen to her. She hadn't anticipated meeting someone like Nathan Jonah Hickey. She simply couldn't allow herself to start having feelings for him—she just couldn't! Dare she risk the possibility of falling into a similar situation as her sisters? Her self-willed spirit and stubborn pride demanded that she set the proper example in the family to show her sisters something. She wanted to prove that she would marry someone saved, prominent, and educated that could provide for his family as if she needed more wealth!

She abruptly stood and Nathan rose immediately afterwards displaying proper manners while Jack and Robert slurped coffee from their china cups. Everyone took notice. "I desire to be excused." Moving swiftly, she exited the dining room. Nathan spoke politely, "Thank you all for your company and the delicious supper and I'd like to be excused."

Of course Mama Mae had to say something, "Did you enjoy yourself?"

"Yes ma'am. I did indeed."

"If you're not doing anything tomorrow, why don't you join us again for Sunday supper?" Before he could respond, she gestured with her hands held up and explained, "I know you don't like to go to church and I'm not one to try and force you. That's between you and God."

He glanced at everyone, "I'll give it some thought. Good night," and then he exited the dining room. Mr. John excused himself to escort him to the front verandah as they both retrieved their hats from the oak hall tree and stand as they passed by it. Mary Ellen peered at them from atop the staircase landing albeit she went unnoticed.

Mr. John patted his back. "I see you've taken fancy to Little Stockings."

He looked at Mr. John responsively as furrows appeared in his forehead, "I feel out of sorts here. I don't think that I'm the kind of man that she desires—much less deserves."

"You need to make a mash on that girl. What that young filly needs is a good strong hardworking buck like you. She don't need some fancy dude stepping up in here. We've all seen enough of that! Ben sure liked you. I wish he was still around."

Nathan relaxed his countenance with a smile. "I loved him too. He was the only father figure that I've had in a while."

He patted Mr. John and said, "Good night." As he stepped down a couple of stairs he turned around and lifted his hand. "Thanks for cleaning the fish."

Mr. John waved his hand downward. "No problem." Nathan pivoted and then journeyed in the direction of the carriage house. He told himself that he just might consider the second invitation to supper.

Mary Ellen desired to know what they had spoken out on the front verandah especially whether Nathan had mentioned anything about her. She rushed to her window and watched him stroll to the carriage house, which was his living quarters as the pole lighting on the property displayed his silhouette in motion.

There was one thing that she knew with a certainty; she wasn't going to allow herself to fall asleep on the floor again. Mary Ellen wasn't sleepy. She opened her vanity by lifting the looking-glass and didn't see what she wanted. She snatched opened the first drawer of the chest-of-drawers, retrieved a fountain pen and journal, pulled up her chair at her desk, and wrote another poem. She was relieved that she didn't have to return downstairs to retrieve pen and paper from the mahogany secretary or in the study.

Mama Mae had positioned herself on the davenport as Marva and Mae relaxed on the matching chaise and chair in the parlor. Robert had gone for the evening. Marva didn't bother to see him to the door for obvious reasons. She realized that she made some mistakes by not waiting on the Lord. Mae too realized the awful truth that she should've waited as well. Jack had gone upstairs to bed unnoticed.

Mama Mae retrieved a hairpin from her bouffant style hair and used it to scratch an annoying itch on her scalp. "Supper was sure good 'specially that catfish that Nate caught. That young man is sure some adventurer."

Mae unlatched her ankle boots and propped her stocking feet on the footstool. She spoke softly and meddlesome as she bruited about Nathan's affection for Mary Ellen. "Mama, I think our singing cowboy has an eye for Little Stockings. Don't you think so Big Stockings?"

Marva was in another world. Mae popped her with her fingers, "Big Stockings! You hear what I said?"

Marva drew a deep breath and released heated frustration. "Don't you think you've done enough gossiping for the day? You need to get a job working for the—Mama what's the name of that newspaper that colored man started up in Washington, D.C.?"

Mae withdrew. "Oh hush girl! I wasn't trying to start nothing. I was just saying that I think Nate likes Little Stockings."

Mama Mae interrupted sharply as her eyes peered over her reading spectacles, "And if he does, what's wrong with that?"

Mae shrugged her shoulders and dropped her head while a sheepish look appeared on her face. She didn't get the gossipy response from the women that she heartily desired. "Nothing, I guess. I just thought you'd like to know."

Mama Mae folded her newspaper and scooted to the edge of the davenport as her countenance took on a serious expression, which everyone knew what that meant. She was the fiery one.

"Let me tell you girls something—." Marva interrupted before she could finish and flung her hands up in a defensive position, "Mama I ain't in it. Mae started this one! I've been seriously thinking about getting my own life right with God and—."

Mama Mae placed her hand outward to signal her to stop talking, "You just need to do that and don't interrupt me again when I'm speaking." She quickly regained her composure and continued as she pointed her finger in the direction of the carriage house.

"There ain't nothing wrong with that boy out there. He's a nice polite young man. Your father told me so and I seen it for myself. I've been praying for him to give his life to God and if he chooses to court Little Stockings, so be it! Now what do you have to say about that?"

Mae continued to look sheepish while Marva nodded in agreement. Mae finally lifted her head and responded once again in a sheepish and somewhat embarrassed tone, "I'll be praying for him too."

Mama Mae concluded, "Now I'm going to bed so that I can be ready on time for church in the morning." Marva looked upon Mae with an expression that clearly denoted that she was staying out of it.

Mary Ellen heard them coming up the stairs. She waited a bit and then went downstairs. As she ventured farther, she could hear voices proceeding from the kitchen area. It was Mr. John. He was seated at the kitchen table enjoying another helping of peach cobbler along with Mr. Pope. The ladies had returned to their quarters for the evening.

"I hope we weren't making too much noise." Mr. Pope smiled. He was a strong-built man in his early fifties and light-skinned. He lost his wife years ago. He's been with the family since and never remarried. Benjamin met him at a rodeo and hired him to work on the ranch.

Mary Ellen smiled and hugged him. "You're alright Mr. Pope. How's everything going? Miss Beatrice outdid herself again on that cobbler."

He smiled again. "She sure did."

"Why didn't you join us at supper?"

He swallowed some cobbler and took a sip of coffee. "Oh I decided to eat right here with the ladies. I'd rather be alone with two lovely ladies any day than to be in a room filled with people." They chuckled.

This time, Mr. John chimed in, "Pay no attention to Mr. Pope. I gather that you came down here for a reason young lady. What's on your mind?"

Before she responded, Mr. Pope got up from the table. "John, I'm going to head back and get some rest." He rinsed his dirty dishes in the sink and then proceeded toward the side door.

"Take it easy now," Mr. John beckoned with his hand raised.

"Good night Mr. Pope." Mary Ellen smiled.

He returned the smile and said, "Good night baby."

Mr. John patted his hand on a chair seat. "Have a seat. Want some coffee?"

She nodded, "Oh no—not this late!"

He looked at her and rubbed his chin, "I'm waiting."

"Oh uh—I was just wondering how Nathan's doing. I saw you both out on the verandah earlier."

Mr. John peered at her and chuckled. "You two are a mess. I don't know what I'm going to do with you young people."

She chuckled and then raised her head while twirling her fingers through her locks. "Did he mention anything about me when you were talking?"

He took a sip of coffee. "You know something—you two remind me of Ben and Mae when they were young. Ben was young and brash. They both liked each other and instead of just admitting the truth of the matter, they both hemmed and hawed until they finally realized what was meant to be. You both could save yourselves a lot of time you know."

Mary Ellen's brows rose. "Did he tell you that he liked me or is that your assumption?"

"No he didn't tell me he liked you. He didn't have to. But what he did mention was that he didn't think you'd be interested in a man like him."

She rested her elbows on the table, which was unheard of in the Beauford household and clasped her hands on the sides of her face in frustration. She spoke firmly, "Mr. John, I didn't graduate from college to end up marrying a ranchman. I want someone saved that's educated like me and that can support me—you know a man with a dream and a goal like daddy."

Mr. John gave her a look of disbelief. He placed his coffee cup down and then looked steadily into her eyes as his countenance changed to a serious expression. He chided, "Young lady, I knew Ben well enough to know that if he heard such trash come out of your mouth he'd take a switch and tear your hind parts up. Ben came from nothing and he made something of himself. If it wasn't for him, you'd all been dressed in rags and no doubt scrubbing somebody's floor or picking cotton!"

Her eyes enlarged and welled with water because she had never heard him speak to her in that manner as she replied, "Daddy wouldn't spank me at this age."

He sipped more coffee. "You needn't forget where God brought you from. You see where that attitude got your sisters. Big Stockings got a man that only wants in for the money and Big Mae married a man that only married her in hopes to get his hands on the Beauford wealth!"

She blotted her eyes with her finger and sniffed. "How does mama feel about that?"

He retorted, "Your mama knows full well what's going on. Y'all don't fool her none."

She straightened herself. "I'd better get some rest so that I can get ready for church in the morning." She scooted her chair out and got up to walk away and he rose from his seat. As she turned around, he spoke, "Little Stockings, just pray. God will guide you through it."

Chapter Five

Mary Ellen stepped out on the second floor front verandah to see whether Mr. John had driven the Sunday carriage around the front of the mansion. It was a four-passenger open-top carriage with steel wheels. Sometimes they used the covered buggy or the *runabout* if only a couple of passengers were riding that they kept in the carriage house. After spotting the carriage, she retrieved her Sunday Bible, fan, drawstring purse, lace gloves, and then proceeded downstairs.

Mary Ellen had pin-curled her hair before she fell asleep last night. Her hair was pulled upward in a bouffant style with a few curly twists that draped down her back. Faux roses encircled her coiffure. Her millinery was wide-brimmed embellished with faux flowers and plumage. Mary Ellen's powder-blue floor-length dress had extra large bouffant short sleeves that tapered slightly above her elbows. The dress had a small cinch waist with added help from her corset. Her springtime lace gloves were long and nearly covered her arms except where her sleeves tapered slightly above her elbows. The skirted portion of her dress flared with faux magnolias sewn around the lower portion. A large fancy bow embellished the dress that tied in the back and draped downward. She looked like a southern belle for certain. A silk choker with a small cross hung around her neck. A matching parasol hung from her right arm along with her drawstring bag and shawl as she clutched her Bible and fan in the left.

It was approaching the ninth hour when Mary Ellen proceeded slowly down the stairs of the verandah and was surprised to see Nathan positioned in the driver's seat of the carriage. He stepped down and studied her in admiration as she approached the carriage. His eyes denoted that she looked exquisite. She paused a moment as their eyes met.

He gently lifted his cowboy hat. "Morning Miss."

"Uh, good morning. What happened to Mr. John?"

A puzzled expression crossed his face until he realized why she asked the question. "I've been driving the family to church on Sundays since your father hired me because Mr. John always drives your mother to town."

Her mouth opened slightly. "Oh, I hadn't realized."

He extended his hand to assist her. "You look very lovely today Miss."

She smiled and replied, "Why thank you."

His eyes lit up and he smiled.

"You called me Mary Ellen when you asked me to read my poem to you."

He thought she was offended and explained, "I meant no disrespect Miss. I'll–."

She gently touched his hand. "I'd like for you to call me Mary Ellen. You're the only one around here that calls me by my real name and I appreciate that."

His eyes twinkled as his beautiful smile reemerged.

Mary Ellen blurted, "I wrote another poem last night."

His heart sang within as he spoke calmly, "I'd like to hear your poem,–that is if you'd care to share it with me."

She smiled while staring into his eyes. "Of course." She curled up her bottom lip nervously and tightened her brows. "Nathan do you mind if I ask you a question?"

He approached her closer, which made her more nervous because he peered directly into her eyes. "Go right ahead."

She cleared her throat. "Why is it that you don't attend church services? The others do."

He lowered his head as he dreaded to tell her the truth of the matter.

"Don't you believe in God?"

He raised his head and resumed his fixation upon her. "Of course. It's just that—well it's complicated. You wouldn't understand."

The remainder of the family exiting the front door with Mae taking the lead suddenly interrupted them. She looked at Nathan and whispered, "We'll talk later." She didn't want Mae's inquisitiveness to interfere. He assisted her into the carriage.

"Morning Nate," Mae stood awaiting him to assist her while Jack stood beside her.

He nodded, "Morning ma'am. Morning sir." Jack returned the gesture. Nathan didn't budge because he refused to assist her into the carriage while her husband stood by idle. Nathan strongly disapproved of lazy slothful men. Mae looked at Jack who wasn't paying any attention to her at first until she grunted. He understood what that meant. "Oh uh, let me help you up."

Mary Ellen was seated in the front and she noticed a look of disgust on Nathan as he watched Jack's reaction. Nathan glanced at Mary Ellen and realized that she noticed so he winced at her. They both smiled and of course, Mae tried to figure out what she missed.

Nathan positioned himself in the driver's seat, grabbed the reins, and directed the team of horses to proceed in the direction of *Mount Holy Hilltop Church* named for its location on the hilltop.

Marva traveled in a separate carriage with Robert and not for romantic reasons. She arranged for Robert to pick her up. She made a decision to give him an ultimatum and didn't want any interference from anyone—especially Mae.

Mama Mae was already at church. She usually arrived early to help out. Therefore, she rode with Mr. Pope, Miss Beatrice, and Miss Edna.

The choir had finished singing their last hymnal for today's service. Everyone resumed their seated positions as they had previously stood to rejoice in the Lord and sway to the melodic sounds of the hymnals, the pipe organ, and tambourines. The Beaufords donated the proceeds to purchase the magnificent pipe organ when Benjamin was alive.

Mary Ellen noticed that Marva wasn't seated in the choir stand this morning. She looked around and squinted because Marva was seated alone a few rows behind her. She wondered where Robert was as there wasn't any sign of his presence. She caught Marva's attention as their eyes met. She asked silently with her lips moving, "Where's Robert?"

Marva raised her brows and shrugged her shoulders with her hands raised to gesture that she didn't know. Mary Ellen's brows tightened again as she was puzzled as to what had taken place. By this time, it was too late for her to question Marva further because Bishop E.G. Bronnum had proceeded to the pulpit. She straightened herself on the pew in the direction of the pulpit.

Mary Ellen primarily focused her attention on Bishop E.G. Bronnum, as he was known for his fiery preaching. He was somewhat of a large build with a deep brown complexion. As she reached for her fan she noticed some of the brethren eyeing her one in particular—Brother Lawrence Trotter. She paused briefly and then returned her attention to Bishop Bronnum.

Although Mary Ellen was attractive, she was cautious and speculative because the Beauford family's prosperity was widely known. She often reminded herself of Benjamin's warnings to her about becoming prey to men. Benjamin had often wished that he had similar talks with the other two sisters. Once he realized that it was too late, he didn't want to make the same mistake with her.

Brother Trotter's focus remained on Mary Ellen with occasional glances at Bishop Bronnum. Lawrence was considered middle-class as his father owned a successful feed store. He was somewhat tall and lanky-built with a light-brown complexion and wavy brown hair. A few of the young single sisters in the church were drawn to him. They were unaware that he had other plans on his mind.

Occasionally Mary Ellen would wave her hand in the air as she was moved within as the preaching soothed her mind and spirit. Her heart was touched by the sermon titled *The Humility of Jesus.* As Bishop Bronnum continued to preach, she rationalized concerning Nathan and the fact that he was unsaved. She earnestly desired for God to give her strength and wisdom to guide her through this.

After the dismissal, parishioners greeted one another with handshakes, smiles, hugs, and kisses along with occasional commentary regarding their thoughts of the sermon. Mary Ellen prepared to make her way toward Marva until she observed Lawrence Trotter greeting Mama Mae. She couldn't hear their conversation as she continued to inch her way to Marva.

Lawrence gave Mama Mae a firm handshake and a generous smile. He conveyed his heart's desire to her. "Mother Beauford with respect, I'd like to request your permission to court your lovely daughter Little Stockings." Mama Mae was taken aback as her eyes enlarged and her facial muscles retracted. She withdrew her hand from his and then clasped her hands as she responded, "Well Brother Trotter, that's up to Little Stockings, so you'd have to ask her yourself."

It wasn't the exact response that he had hoped for. He explained, "Ma'am my reason for asking your permission is because Brother Beauford's gone on and now you're in charge of Little Stockings."

Mama Mae placed her hand on his shoulder and peered into his eyes, "Little Stockings is in charge of herself and I hear what you're saying—but what I'm saying to you is—you need to address her yourself 'cause I'm leaving that decision to her." She stepped away, retrieved her Bible and belongings from the pew, and continued to fellowship with other parishioners.

"What happened to Robert?" Mary Ellen finally made her way over to where Marva was standing. Marva frowned.

"Girl I finally put my foot down!" An expression of surprise left Mary Ellen speechless for a moment and then she finally spoke.

"Wha—what happened? I didn't think you had it in you to be strong."

Marva released a slight huff. "I can't keep disgracing myself. That's why I didn't sing in the choir today. It's like mama said. I can't be doing my dirt and then brushing the crumbs off my face as if nothing happened."

Her eyes welled with tears and Mary Ellen hugged her as she cried. "I just can't keep letting him take advantage of me. I asked him this morning when we were going to set a date and he said the same thing that he always says. So I told him that it was over and let me out at church."

"I was wondering why I didn't see him this morning."

She sniffed and mopped her face with her glove.

"Here I have a handkerchief in my purse." Mary Ellen retracted the drawstrings and retrieved an embroidered cotton handkerchief then handed it to her. "Come let me take you to the altar and have bishop pray for you."

"Okay," she sniffed again and went for prayer.

Lawrence had prepared to approach Mary Ellen during that moment but he soon realized that his timing was off. Afterwards, they exited the church and Mary Ellen noticed that Mr. John was there waiting to drive them home. He had driven alone to church and decided to wait to see who needed a ride back. He drove Mary Ellen, Mae, Marva, and Jack. Mama Mae returned with Mr. Pope, Miss Beatrice, and Miss Edna.

Mary Ellen changed into one of her long spring dresses. It was a pastel pink color. She removed the faux rosettes from her hair and allowed it to drape loosely around her shoulders. She decided to sit outside on the front verandah. She had taken the poem that she had recently written. Marva sat on the back verandah, as she desired to be alone. The others were inside having a late lunch.

Mary Ellen placed some sandwiches and fruit in a basket and brought out a pitcher of water along with two glasses. She desired to take another ride on Rain albeit there had been no sign of Nathan. She assumed that he was either visiting in town or perhaps napping. She hoped to see him to finish their conversation from earlier.

Mary Ellen looked up and noticed a horse-drawn buggy being driven from the road proceeding from the west, which is the direction that they travel to church. She stood and placed her hand against her brows to block the sun so that she could see farther. She squinted and still had no idea as to who the traveler was. She slowly proceeded to the wrought-iron gate and waited. As the buggy drew nearer, she felt a sunken feeling in her empty stomach. It was Lawrence Trotter from church. She wondered whether he was coming to visit her or perhaps to speak to Mama Mae.

He lighted from the buggy and approached the gate. He was still dressed in his Sunday church suit. "Nice afternoon." He removed his trilby from his head and clutched it in his hands.

She opened the gate to let him in. "Oh you must be here to see Mama. I saw you talking with her at church this morning. I'll let her know you're here."

Before she could advance farther he interrupted, "Little Stockings, I'm here to see you."

She drew a deep breath and prepared herself mentally for what she anticipated to proceed from his being. "You see I spoke to Mother Beauford this morning about courting you and she told me that I had to speak to you, which I thought was highly unusual. Yep—highly unusual. So I'm asking your permission to court you."

Mary Ellen's mouth flung open albeit she was speechless. She had a gut feeling that he had spoken to Mama Mae concerning her because he kept staring at her during service. He followed her as she proceeded to the verandah and sat on the swing. "So what's your answer? I need to know because I've got plans."

Mary Ellen looked up at him as he stood in front of her. She noticed that he was slightly shorter than her. She hunched her brows and mirrored his word, "Plans?"

Mama Mae approached the door to see who had dropped by to visit. She believed it to be one of the sisters from church that occasionally drops by on Sundays for supper. Upon seeing that it was Lawrence, she immediately knew why he was there. She tried to ease away from the door without him noticing her. But it was too late.

"Good afternoon Mother Beauford." His voice sounded as if he was acting for a stage play.

Mama Mae had a withdrawn expression, "I didn't expect to see you so soon."

Before she could walk away from the door, he felt the need to impress them as if he had rehearsed prior to his arrival. He stood back on his legs and rocked then boasted as if he was addressing an audience, "I'm a young entrepreneur. You see I've started my own business—yes *indeedy*. My father lent me the money to get it started and one of these days," he tugged on his suspenders, "I'm going to have a spread like this—yep," he nodded and grinned.

They were annoyed by his self-aggrandizing braggadocio. Mary Ellen didn't know what to make of this spectacle. She turned and glanced at Mama Mae who was speechless, which was unusual for her. Mary Ellen poured water into one of the glasses and sipped while he continued to express himself.

"I was just asking Little Stockings for permission to court her."

Mary Ellen gulped water and this time Mama Mae spoke up, "Well son, what'd she say?"

He looked at Mary Ellen and explained, "She hasn't said much of anything yet ma'am. I gather that she's still thirsty seeing how she keeps drinking that water."

Mary Ellen restrained herself from laughing until her insides ached. She was unaware that Nathan had approached. He stood on the steps and glanced at Lawrence and then Mary Ellen. When she noticed him her countenance fell.

"Afternoon Mary Ellen," he spoke and lifted his cowboy hat gesturing toward her.

She spoke, "Good Afternoon."

Lawrence extended his hand and Nathan gave him a firm handshake as his eyes remained focused on Mary Ellen and then he noticed the paper with the poem. Mama Mae had taken this opportunity to ease away from the door and returned to what she was doing.

"Lawrence Trotter here and what's your name sir?" He smiled.

"Nathan Hickey." He didn't return the smile.

Nathan had the remainder of the day off and he had purposed to see her. He looked forward to visiting Mary Ellen since he last spoke to her earlier that morning.

Lawrence roared, "I just stopped by because I've been trying to get this little lady to allow me to court her and she just keeps drinking that water."

Nathan looked at Lawrence as his eyes filled with disappointment albeit he was calm. He questioned, "Any luck?"

Lawrence chuckled, "I don't believe in luck. But if you'd like to know whether she said yes, I believe she'll come around to it. You see I got my own feed business and all and I look forward to having myself a spread like this here someday."

Mary Ellen was filled with disappointment and embarrassment as it manifested in her countenance. She believed that Lawrence had ruined her chance to try to get

Nathan to open up to her. She desperately desired to know what was bothering him and then it hit her. She reminded herself about what she said about desiring a man that had a goal, was saved, and could support her. Lawrence had the right fit but she found him to be irritating and seemingly in love with himself. She tried to picture a life with him sitting around talking about himself and realized that what she really desired was true love.

Nathan looked at Mary Ellen and sensed that she didn't seem like herself. He became frustrated and spoke up. "I think that I'll go for a ride on *Midnight*."

Mary Ellen didn't want him to take the horseback ride without her. She just had to think of some polite way to rid herself of this Lawrence character. She finally spoke up just as Nathan had turned to depart. "Nathan wait!"

Nathan was awestruck! He stopped on the second stair step and turned around. He seized the moment and chose to relax in Benjamin's former favorite chair while Lawrence stood there with a look of bemusement. Lawrence released a nervous chuckle then spoke, "I suppose I'd better head back. Besides, I've got some business deals to check on. Good day to you both."

He walked away, climbed inside the buggy, and proceeded in a westward direction. Mama Mae crept to the door unnoticed as she heard him leaving and noticed

Nathan sitting on the verandah. She smiled and then walked away.

Nathan had removed his cowboy hat and placed it on the railing. They smiled at one another, as they were relieved from the distraction. Mary Ellen studied him as he was dressed in dark blue denim waist overalls with black leather suspenders attached to the suspender buttons. He wore a twill-striped western cowboy shirt with metal closures. She could smell his after-shave. It reminded her of when he sat at the dining table across from her.

"You told me that you wrote another poem. Let's hear it."

She slowly recited the poem while he listened attentively.

"This one is titled: *My Life in Retrospect.*
Thought I'd take a moment of my life to reflect,
O'er reasons to praise rather than feel regret.
Thank You Lord for grass, flowers, and the big oak tree,
I truly thank You utmost for saving someone like me.
You've kept me from danger lurking around,
Elevated my feet to a safe higher ground.
My heaviness of heart has truly been lifted,
By your bountiful blessings I'm wondrously gifted.
Your gentle voice so soothing and calm,

My hurtful wounds healed by Your sweet balm.
I looked through my window at the stars that formed a
constellation,
That You spoke into existence without restraint or
reservation.
They sparkle in the galaxy in all their resplendence,
As they glorify You from a far greater distance.
Your presence is better than silver and fine gold,
For it is Your hand that has kept me on this road."

He smiled, nodded, and said, "Nice—real nice."

"Thank you." Mary Ellen wanted to continue their conversation from earlier. Now was as good a time as any. She decided to take the risk. Her countenance changed from a smile to a look of concern.

"I asked you why you didn't like to attend church services and you told me that I wouldn't understand. I'd like to try to understand if you would share it with me."

He poured water from the pitcher into the remaining glass, took a swallow, and placed his glass beside hers on the table. He drew a deep breath and released it. His eyes looked downward instead of in hers. He spoke slowly as his eyes appeared to be glassy. "The only one that I've ever shared this with was Mr. Beauford and he kept quiet about it. We used to go riding sometimes and talk and have lunch together."

He drew another deep breath and paused. Mary Ellen placed her hands over his and gave a gentle squeeze. She felt the roughness of his palms and noticed that his hands were much larger than hers. "I'd like for you to feel comfortable in sharing this with me. You need to trust someone. You trusted daddy and I'm sure he didn't disappoint you."

"Only when he passed away because I had no one to talk to. He was a good man. He was like a father to me."

He took another gulp of water. "My folks were—my father was a minister and my mother was a missionary. They'd take me to church services and their tent meetings when they had them. They had strong faith in God and He—He let me—I mean them down."

His eyes brimmed with tears. He removed a blue neckerchief from around his neck and wiped his face. His eyes had reddened. She held his hands taut. She spoke, "Finish."

"They were murdered right in the church. I didn't know where I was going to live. I didn't know what to do until I met your father. He offered me a job here and let me move in the carriage house and I've been struggling with this ever since. I've been saving my wages because I planned to leave my job here and track them down and—."

Her eyes filled with tears. "And what Nathan?"

He looked at her while a serious expression shrouded him. He spoke firmly, "Avenge my people."

Tears flowed from her eyes, as this was much worse than she had anticipated. Mary Ellen didn't know whether she was strong enough to handle it. She lowered her head and murmured, "Oh Jesus."

He lowered his head. "And now that I met you things have changed. I'm confused. I had it all figured out—what my plans were and now—."

She interrupted, "Look at me."

He lifted his head and looked into her eyes. She entreated him. "You don't need to throw away your life going after these people. Your parents were saved and they wouldn't want anything to happen to you. They wouldn't want you to do something like this. Vengeance belongs to the Lord."

Her words were soothing. He spoke gently, "I realize that. My mother gave me the middle name Jonah because she wanted me to become a minister someday in my father's stead. And after they were killed, I found myself resenting that name."

He regained his composure and spoke candidly, "There's something that I need to say to you."

She feared somewhat but still desired to know what he had to say. "What is it?"

"I love you Mary Ellen. I'm sure of it. I have since we were introduced and you could barely speak to me."

Before she could gather her thoughts, he lifted her chin slightly and sweetly kissed her lips ever so gently. Afterwards, she read his lips as he told her that he loved her again without uttering a sound. Her eyes enlarged as she peered at him. He reached over, poured more water into her glass, and placed it to her lips. She took a deep gulp.

He felt somewhat guilty and explained, "I shouldn't have done that. I apologize. I should go. I've laid a lot on your shoulders and you don't deserve my pain. Maybe you should give that Lawrence fella an answer." He stood and quickly exited the verandah.

Mary Ellen leaned over and wept into her hands. She didn't know what to do at this point. She didn't want the others to hear her so she forced herself to regain her composure. She eyed the sandwiches in the basket, tore them into small pieces, and flung them over the verandah for the birds to eat. Mary Ellen started to return inside and she had a change of heart. She desired to be alone and meditate on the Lord. She left everything on the verandah and set out to take a long walk on the property.

Chapter Six

Mary Ellen didn't see any signs of Nathan as she ventured past the stables, the cattle, and the carriage house. She believed that he was purposely ignoring her and therefore chose not to remove Rain from the stables. She continued to walk and talk to God audibly.

"Lord I truly need You to bless in this situation. I don't know how I feel about Nathan. All I know is that he needs to be saved before he does something crazy and I don't want anything to happen to him." She sniffed and continued.

"Lord, why couldn't things have been different between us? If his parents had never been killed, things would probably be different. He'd probably be saved and I could've—." She suddenly stopped as she told herself that had things been different they would never have met.

Mary Ellen noticed a small twig lying on the ground. She tossed it then grabbed the sides of her dress and spun around once then continued walking. Mary Ellen hadn't realized just how far she had ventured because she was near *Beauford Brook.*

Upon reaching the brook, she decided to unfasten her stockings from her garter and slip her feet into the water. She rested on a large rock and swished her feet in the water. Mary Ellen became dismayed to the point that she didn't care about risking ruining her lovely dress. She leaned back and talked to the Lord again.

"Lord do all relationships have to be complicated? All I want is a nice saved husband that loves me and not be selfish and self-centered. Someone humble like Bishop Bronnum preached about this morning." She began to reverie on the morning sermon regarding humility as she withdrew her feet from the brook and closed her eyes.

Mary Ellen wasn't paying attention to her surroundings as she had just started to get in a relaxed state of mind and drifted off to sleep. She rested a while and was suddenly awakened by a sound. She opened her eyes then sat up and looked around as her lips started trembling. A thirty-six inch water moccasin was camouflaged in the vegetation beside her. It had spotted her and its tail began to vibrate. Mary Ellen tried not to panic as she slowly eased herself up so that she could run. When she started to run, she slipped on the wet rock and fell down near the vegetation. Moreover, just when she thought that she was going to be bitten, she observed rocks being hurled at the snake and it became motionless.

Mary Ellen looked up to see who threw the rocks and was surprised to see that it was Nathan. She was happy to see him and tried to get up again and felt soreness. She didn't realize that her foot had been cut on the rock as blood oozed from the wound. Nathan kneeled, lifted her in his arms, and placed her on the ground away from danger. He removed his neckerchief and bound her wound.

She looked at him in bemusement. "How'd you know that I was here?"

"I didn't. This is where I go when I need to get away. I usually come here to fish on the weekends. I saw something pink and wondered what it was. And when I got up to take a look, I was surprised to see that it was your dress and you were asleep. I started not to disturb you until I noticed the water moccasin and that's when I grabbed some rocks and started throwing them."

Mary Ellen felt stupid and ashamed as she released a sigh. "I apologize for ruining your day off." She lifted her right hand in frustration and continued, "First it was me questioning you about something that you didn't want to share with me and now this! And now I've made a mess of your whole day." Her eyes welled with tears as she tried to say more.

He looked up and whistled. His horse trotted over to where they were and he gently lifted her up on it. She asked, "Aren't you going to get on with me? What about your fishing pole?"

"You should head back and I'll *ride Shank's mare* with my plunder when I'm done. Have Mr. John to put Midnight in the stables for me." She looked bewildered because she didn't understand.

He explained, "I'll walk." He patted his horse and yelled, "Yaw!" Midnight always obeyed him.

Mary Ellen wanted to turn back, ride toward Nathan, and sit at the edge of the brook with him. A spirit of rejection coated her mind. She wished she had never given Nathan the time of day. Nevertheless, at the same token she was glad that he was there to save her from being bitten. She's seen people that were extremely swollen and ill with deep red blotches from being bitten. She resented the fact that Nathan seemed to have withdrawn himself from her. However, he told her that he loved her. Mary Ellen hoped that she still meant something to him. There had to be a ray of hope lying somewhere—but where?

Mary Ellen considered giving up on him as guilt ate away at her heart. If she gives up so easily where is her faith in God? She couldn't believe that he told her to give Lawrence an answer. She wasn't interested in Lawrence because she realized that his presence alone was enough to frustrate her.

Mr. John couldn't believe his eyes as he assisted her off Midnight. "Girl what have you been doing—crawling through mud and where are your stockings and shoes?"

Mary Ellen felt foolish and released a huff. "I was sitting by the brook and a water moccasin tried to bite me and Nathan came out of nowhere and saved me. And as for my stockings and shoes I left them by the brook." She rolled her eyes upward.

He leaned over and slapped his right knee while laughing. After regaining his composure he responded, "He did go fishing and he seemed a little upset about something or another. He didn't say what."

"Who cares?" Mary Ellen announced frustratingly with her hands on her hips.

"Don't sass me Little Stockings. What y'all do have a lovers' quarrel?"

Mary Ellen frowned. She looked at him for a moment. "Mr. John, do you know what I admire about you the most?"

"Admire?" His brows rose.

"Yes—admire. I admire the fact that you mean exactly what you say."

He stroked Midnight and replied, "I reckon I don't see the need to hem and haw 'cause it's a waste of time."

Mr. John had a great deal of wisdom and experience. He glanced at the neckerchief tied around her foot and knew that it belonged to Nathan.

"It's just a small cut," she explained. "Nathan carried me away from danger although I could've walked."

He smiled and spoke, "One of these days he's going to carry you across the threshold."

Her eyes squinted and she patted his shoulder. "Take care Mr. John. Oh Nathan would like for you to put Midnight in the stables for him."

She turned and walked away.

Mr. John yelled, "Have Miss Beatrice to put some salve on that cut."

She smiled as she stood on the rear verandah. "Okay."

Mary Ellen had refreshed herself and changed. She sat in the same seat at the dining table as she had done when Nathan dined with the family. She wasn't up to having the usual enlightening conversations with the family. Jack was the only man at the table and he usually didn't have much to say. Jack didn't do much of anything. He didn't work or help out with anything on the property.

Mary Ellen prayed that no one would bring up the subject of Nathan. She simply wanted to eat and afterwards sit on the front verandah and collect her thoughts. It just didn't seem like the Sundays that she remembered before she started college. They used to have lively discussions and people over for supper. Most importantly, her father was present. Mary Ellen tried very hard not to regret ever leaving because she wished that she had spent those final years with her father and the family.

Mae couldn't resist being talkative at the dining table or any place else. "I haven't seen Little Stockings since church this morning. Why are you so quiet over there?"

Mae leaned at the dining table so that she could view Mary Ellen. "Is everything alright? Did I miss something when I took my afternoon nap?"

Mama Mae sliced a piece of freshly baked bread and spread butter on it. "Now leave Little Stockings alone. She's had quite some day." She tore a piece from her bread and then resumed speaking, "You know Brother Trotter at church?"

Mae felt a story coming forth that she could latch onto. "What about him?"

Mama Mae slid her bread across her plate as it soaked some gravy and took a bite. Between chewing and swallowing she answered, "Well, he asked Little Stockings for her hand in courtship."

This drew Marva and Mae's attention. Jack peered intently as his ears seemed to perk. He's been around Mae too long and was beginning to pick up her inquisitive spirit.

Mae exclaimed, "Why he's certainly no esquire. And speaking of esquire, where's Nate? I thought he was invited for supper?"

Mama Mae spoke with her eyes peering up at Mae, "Now he's what you'd call an esquire."

Mary Ellen dreaded the fact that they brought up the subject of Nathan. She fluttered her lashes as her eyes brimmed with tears. She forced herself to be strong and not fall apart at that moment. They dined on the remaining catfish that Nathan had caught.

Mary Ellen stuck her fork in the catfish and was reminded of Nathan. She missed seeing him sit across from her at the dining table. She resented questioning him about his past. If only she hadn't. Mary Ellen tried to understand whether she was simply infatuated with the handsome cowboy or whether she actually had feelings for him. Having never been involved in a relationship before made her inexperienced in ascertaining what she actually felt.

Mae looked at Mary Ellen and asked, "Do you plan on letting Brother Trotter court you?"

Mary Ellen answered frustratingly without looking up from her plate, "He isn't my type."

Mama Mae added, "That *youngin* needs to slow down. He's sure some fast talker."

Mary Ellen looked at her mother, "Mama I did everything possible to keep from laughing at him. I did my utmost to be polite."

Everyone laughed including Jack. The laughter helped Mary Ellen to develop a cheerful countenance. She didn't have much of an appetite at first because she was upset. She was able to finish her meal, as she hadn't eaten anything all day.

After supper, Mary Ellen stretched out on the swing on the front verandah, opened her small Bible, and silently read some passages of Scriptures. One in particular that she chose to read audibly was Psalm 31:24.

"Be of good courage, and he shall strengthen your heart, all ye that hope in the LORD."

She felt much better as she clutched her Bible to her bosom and rocked the swing with her foot. Mary Ellen was certainly glad that her family didn't get overly carried away with their inquisitions.

Mary Ellen didn't want to be like the others with no profession and just lie around the mansion all day gossiping and doing nothing. She received her education and wanted to put it to good use—perhaps teach classical literature. If she taught the course at one of the colleges, she would have to leave Beauford Place. After all, nothing seemed to be going right and that idea didn't seem so bad.

She closed her eyes to meditate on the Lord for a while. After the span of approximately ten minutes had passed, she heard a familiar sound of black leather boots on the steps. It was Nathan standing there holding her shoes clasped between two of his fingers.

Her feeling of apprehension prevented her from blurting something offensive. Therefore, she decided to let him speak first. He raised his hat and spoke, "Evening."

Mary Ellen responded, "Good evening." She restrained herself from behaving as if she was happy to see him and therefore acted as if they never had any romantic ties whatsoever; albeit she didn't want to be rude.

He tried to make eye contact with her and she became resilient. She focused her eyes in a distant view farther down the road. Nathan placed her shoes on the floor of the verandah beside her. He peered at her because she didn't look at her shoes. "I cleaned your shoes for you. I don't think that you meant to leave them at the brook."

Mary Ellen sat with her fingers clasped while her hands rested on her stomach as she rocked the swing.

"Thank you." She reached for her shoes then stood and spoke without making eye contact, "I guess I'll bid you goodnight." She left him standing there and returned inside the mansion upstairs to her room.

It was difficult and somewhat painful for her to walk away. She desired to go out on her bedroom verandah but refused because she didn't want him to look up and see her standing there. Therefore, she peered at him from her window as he walked to his dwelling. It was still light outside.

Mary Ellen sat in the rocking chair in her bedroom that was situated next to the fireplace and opened her hope chest. She sifted through a stack of papers until she found what she was looking for. It was an application to become an instructor at her Alma Mater, Oldwood College. Mary Ellen's classical literature professor had grown fond of her and recommended her for an instructor's position. She never shared this information with anyone because during that time she wanted to return to Tradassa Town and be near her loved ones. She had been selected amongst very few people of color as she had graduated at the top of her class.

Uncertainty swept over her in anticipation as to how her family will react. Nevertheless, Mary Ellen completed the application, addressed the envelope, and affixed a three-cent green Washington postage stamp in hopes to mail it in the morning. Mary Ellen considered waiting until she received an official acceptance before informing her family. Her professor explained to her that it would give her an opportunity to meet new people. Her mind was made up and she's the type that can be strong-willed and stubborn as her Aunt Imogene's mule.

Mary Ellen was distraught over the recent events. She never anticipated her first kiss to turn into a disaster. She wanted that moment to be something special. Nevertheless, she did take time to pray earnestly for Nathan, as she didn't want him to ruin his life trying to exact vengeance. She wept in intervals, as she felt sorry concerning his dilemma. She asked herself what she would do if it was her in his situation. She found it difficult to try to fully understand his pain albeit she knows what it's like to lose one parent.

Mary Ellen told herself that she was being a hypocrite because she desires to runaway to escape her problems while she feels that Nathan shouldn't run away but face his problems and forgive those that trespassed against him and his parents. All that she could do at this point was to have faith and be strong as best she could.

Nathan sat with one leg stretched across a footstool while a spirit of frustration enveloped him as he brooded concerning the death of his parents. He leaned and opened a steel safe that was positioned next to his high-back chair. He removed its contents and placed everything on the small wooden table on the opposite side of him. He rummaged through some of the papers until something caught his attention. It was a framed black and white photograph of his parents. They were a lovely couple. Nathan stared at the photograph as he clasped it in his hands. His eyes reddened and tears flowed. His breathing had become heavy until he spoke as if he was addressing his parents while he continued to stare at the photograph. "I don't know what else to do. Everything's gone wrong. I'm not supposed to be here in this situation."

Nathan retrieved another framed photograph. It was a photograph of him when he was a small lad. He was dressed in a suit and hat and clutched a small Bible, which was a gift from his parents. He was happy during that time of his life. He sifted through more of the contents and retrieved a large Bible that once belonged to his father. He opened it and read the inscription. It had been scribed from his grandfather to his father as a gift. He came from a lineage of godly men. Nathan carefully placed the Bible in the safe. Afterwards, he continued to sift through the contents until he found what he had been searching for. It was a newspaper clipping for the nationally renowned Livingston Detective Agency. They were notorious for tracking outlaws as they would go through great lengths to capture the *wanted* lawbreakers. It was either them or he could hire a bounty hunter; only Nathan was dissatisfied to have them track the killers and turn them over to the law. He wanted to hire them to give him a lead on the killers so that he could take matters into his own hands. And then he would finally be at peace—so he believed as the tears stopped flowing and his breathing steadied.

He lifted a .44-caliber ivory-handled revolver from the safe and sat it on the table. His eyes scanned the newspaper clipping and studied every detail concerning the agency. He had read the clipping numerous times since his arrival to Beauford Place. He already had the envelope sealed and planned to mail it in the morning. Nathan leaned over again, reached inside the safe, and retrieved a large metal box. He opened the box and it contained stacks of Silver Certificates, Gold Certificates, gold Liberty Head Eagles, Morgan silver dollars, Indian head pennies, Barber half-dollars, quarters, and dimes. He had more than enough to pay for the agency's services. Nathan inherited the majority of the money from his father. But he refused to use his inheritance to pay the agency fees. He saved his wages from working at Beauford Place to pay the agency.

He asked himself, what about Mary Ellen? He can't become a killer and have any hope of being with her. How did he get himself into this fix? He knows that he's in love with Mary Ellen. And Mama Mae seems to have taken a liking to him. What will he do afterwards? What if there are repercussions? What if he should be killed while trying to requite his parents' deaths? What if the Livingston Detective Agency decides to solve the murders of the men that murdered the Hickeys and trace it back to him?

Nathan frustratingly returned the contents back into the safe and slammed its door shut. He released an exasperating plea. "Lord it's not fair! It's just not fair!"

He grabbed a fountain pen and ripped a sheet of paper from a gummed pad. He walked across the room, grabbed a book, and returned to his chair. He penned a partial poem.

The gentle caress of your hands upon mine;
Bring comfort and sooth my troubled mind.
You please me in a spiritual way that
My heart cannot comprehend.

Afterwards, he crumpled the paper and tossed it into the waste can.

Chapter Seven

Mary Ellen had awakened early as the sun highlighted her room. She chuckled as she listened to Nathan sing while he worked. She realized that he would be missed especially by her should he decide to leave Beauford Place. She told herself that if she left Tradassa Town before Nathan, she wouldn't have time to focus on him. She crept over to the window and observed him tending to the horses. He appeared to be content. She spotted Rain and Midnight. They were the most beautiful of all the horses.

After she bathed and dressed, she snatched the letter and proceeded downstairs. She didn't care whether the rest of the family members had awakened. They usually slept late, which added to Mary Ellen's cause to feel dutiful and honored to teach. One thing that she and Nathan had in common is the fact that they detested slothfulness and laziness.

Mary Ellen proceeded toward the kitchen to see whether Mr. John or Mr. Pope was around. No one was in the kitchen. Mary Ellen was surprised that she had awakened earlier than she realized, as there was no sign of Miss Beatrice either. She opened the back door and stepped out on the verandah. There was no one there. Before she could return inside, Nathan had noticed her as he was riding on Rain in the corral. He stopped singing and waved his hat at her. She waved back and for some reason they both smiled at one another as if nothing ever happened. She hoped to have one of the men drop her letter off in the letterbox. Perhaps Nathan would ride up the road to the letterbox for her as she didn't want to miss the postman.

She grabbed the sides of her yellow calico dress and hastened toward the corral. Her hair was loose and it seemed to fly about her face until she finally reached her destination. She climbed up and stood on one rail of the wooden corral. Nathan had a pleasant expression as he looked at her. He rode Rain over to the side of the corral where she was waiting. He dismounted the mare, climbed on the rail, and faced her. He gently stroked Mary Ellen's hair from her face and spoke, "Morning."

Breathlessly, she spoke, "Good morning. Will you please take this to the letterbox for me? I didn't see Mr. Pope or Mr. John."

He carefully slid the letter inside his leather weskit alongside the letter that he planned to mail that morning. She studied him and noticed that he was dressed in dark denim jeans. She found it difficult to tear herself away from his presence. He had such a drawing affect toward her.

He casually mentioned, "I thought at first that you'd written another poem and came over here to share it with me."

She smiled with a slight chuckle. "No. I'm afraid that I have more important things to write about these days."

A solemn look appeared on his face. "More important than God?"

Her smile abruptly left. "Nothing's more important than God!"

He responded sheepishly, "You're the one that said it. I was just curious as to why you'd say something like that being a God-fearing woman and all."

Her breathing deepened as her eyes appeared as a bull ready to charge. She emphasized, "Will you please take my letter to the letterbox before the postman arrives? It's very important!"

"Sure thing, Miss." He jumped down from the fence and mounted Rain. He rode her toward the opposite end of the corral and let out a loud, "Yaw!" Mary Ellen's eyes enlarged and her heart beat fast as Nathan jumped over a lower section of the corral fence while riding Rain. She gulped while placing her hand across her bosom. She let out an outburst, "He's crazy—absolutely crazy!" She couldn't restrain herself from laughing. Mary Ellen had purposed to just hand him the letter to mail and leave the corral. She glanced over at his horse while making clicking sounds with her voice and teeth in an effort to draw Midnight's attention. She finally called and beckoned with her arm. "Midnight! Come here boy! Come on." Midnight trotted over toward Mary Ellen as she still had her feet propped on the rail. She stroked the horse. "That's a good boy."

Within seconds, Mary Ellen developed a stupid look on her face, which usually spelled trouble. She opened the corral gate, reclosed it, and mounted Midnight without a saddle. She rode Midnight around the corral. She saw Nathan approaching on Rain as the letterbox was just up the road. He spotted her riding Midnight, nodded his head sideways, dismounted Rain, and opened the gate. He led Rain toward her.

Nathan gently grabbed Midnight's reins. Mary Ellen eased back and dismounted. He cautioned her, "Midnight don't take kindly to strangers riding him unless I give the order."

She looked at him in fear. Nathan mounted Midnight and extended his left hand toward Mary Ellen. She paused for a moment and then reached for his hand as he lifted her up on the steed. She fastened her arms around his waist and exited the gate. Nathan dismounted to close the gate. Afterwards, they rode away from the corral. Mary Ellen was distraught at first and then she felt relaxed and safe as the wind traveled through her wild-looking coarse hair. She had desired to take another ride. Nevertheless, she didn't anticipate riding on Midnight with Nathan.

Mary Ellen realized that it was becoming increasingly difficult for her to detach herself from him. She had purposed in her heart to accept the teaching position that was previously offered as she aptly demonstrated by mailing the letter. It became clear to her that she would have to leave if she accepted the position. But he was leaving too and possibly going to wind up in prison or perhaps dead.

They rode to a meadow with lovely wildflowers. After they dismounted, Mary Ellen stared in wonder at the array of wildflowers while Nathan gathered some and handed them to her. She was awestruck!

What was more fascinating is when they observed a whitetail deer nearby. It ran in the opposite direction the moment it sensed their presence. Nathan didn't say anything. He took her hand and led her to a small wooden bridge that Mr. John constructed years ago upon her father's request. They stood on the bridge and leaned against the railing while staring into the water.

Nathan placed his hand atop hers and gently stroked it. Mary Ellen could feel the roughness of his palm. Nevertheless, she didn't mind. He slowly turned her around and placed his arms around her. She peered into his eyes, as they both were speechless. Mary Ellen felt helpless as if she could melt away in his arms. But what about their plans? He leaned to kiss her and she turned her head aside. "Nathan, we're just toying with one another."

He stopped then asked, "What do you mean? I'm serious."

Her lashes fluttered as she looked at him and explained, "We shouldn't play with this. You have plans that don't include me and I have plans that don't include you. We shouldn't become romantically involved because one of us–," she pointed her thumb to herself while she explained, "if not both of us are going to get hurt behind this and I don't want it to be me!"

He withdrew himself but remained in front of her.

She lowered her head in frustration, turned around, and leaned on the bridge railing. She observed a reflection of her long wild-looking wooly-like hair while staring at the water and gasped. He quickly looked down at the water and questioned, "Are you okay? What'd you see?"

She chuckled and looked at him. "I didn't mean to startle you. I just looked at my reflection in the water and realized that I look a sight frightful."

He resumed his serious countenance and gently stroked her hair. "Let me tell you something sweetheart, I don't care how your hair looks. You're every bit as beautiful to me as the day we met."

She tightly gripped the wildflowers and peered into his eyes. "I don't think that you realize the seriousness of everything that I'm trying to say. I uh," she sighed, "I've been thinking about leaving this place. I don't see any reason for me to stay around here anymore. Daddy's gone now and–."

His brows tightened and she paused. He gripped the railing and spoke. "I miss him too. Your father was a great man. I don't think I could've survived if it hadn't been for him. But now he's gone and life goes on. And now it's time for you to move forward."

She listened carefully as she played with the petals on the wildflowers. "That's what I've been trying to tell you. I've decided to move on." She stopped playing with the wildflowers and peered into his eyes. "I've decided to leave Tradassa Town for good. I'm taking an employment position out of state."

She determined from the look of amazement in his eyes that her news wasn't well-received as his heart sunk within. He remained silent for a moment. It appeared as if numerous thoughts clouded his mind. She felt guilty afterwards as tears clouded her eyes.

"It isn't as if you don't already have plans. From what you told me the other day, you plan to commit murder! How far do you think you'll get after that?" She gestured with her arms raised.

His eyes looked glazed as if he was in deep thought and then he finally responded. "You don't understand what I must do. My folks were all I had in this life. I don't have anything else. I don't have a fancy college education like you, although my folks had planned to send me and I don't have a feed business like that Lawrence fella. And I don't want to lie around like Jack. He's a coffee boiler!"

This time Mary Ellen raised her right hand in frustration and waved it downward, "Oh I don't care what you do or what happens to you! If you want to throw away your life then go ahead. I'm sure your folks would've been pleased to know that their only son would someday commit murder!" She tossed the wildflowers into the water, took a few steps, and turned around. "You told me that you loved me and this is what I get—a man that wants to throw away his life. I wished I'd never come back to this place. I should've stayed in Ohio!" She proceeded toward Midnight and stood beside the steed. "Well, aren't you coming?"

He walked over toward her, mounted the steed, and assisted her up. They proceeded back hastily as thoughts seemed to coat their minds. It appeared as if the wind carried them. Nathan couldn't see Mary Ellen's tears flowing while she gripped his waist and she couldn't see his.

They dismounted from Midnight upon their return to the corral. As they looked upon one another with red eyes, their expressions cried out that they both were unhappy with their decisions.

Mary Ellen started to abruptly depart and return to the mansion. However, she chose not to leave just yet. They leaned against the corral and were silent. Mary Ellen finally spoke up. "Why did you approach me from the beginning when you knew all along what you had planned to do? What were you thinking?"

He answered, "I don't know. Your family spoke about you a lot while you were away. I knew that we'd meet someday and I thought you'd be like your sisters and you're not. But what I really didn't know was that I'd fall in love with you. And that's what's hard for me to handle at this point."

She detected the sincerity in his voice. "I understand because I didn't anticipate meeting you. I suppose we both were taken by surprise."

Their eyes were still red as they fought back their tears. They embraced as if they didn't want to let go. Afterwards, Mary Ellen withdrew herself and explained, "Look, I think it would be best if we would just be friends and that way when we leave this place, whichever one of us leaves first, it won't be so painful. Are you alright with that?"

With a sad countenance he responded, "Yes," which was a canard. He knew that he desired to be more than just friends. He opened the gate for her and she returned to the mansion in time for breakfast.

Mary Ellen tied her hair back so that she could look presentable at the dining table and washed her face and hands in the basin. She splashed water in her eyes to alleviate the redness as she didn't want her family to notice.

She could smell the maple syrup before she entered the dining room. The family was just being served. She sat across from Mr. John. Seated beside him were Mae and Jack. Marva and Mama Mae sat beside her. Mr. Pope ate in the kitchen as usual. She realized that Nathan never dined in the house with the exception of the one time when he came for supper.

Whenever Mama Mae prayed for the blessing of the food, she usually incorporated prayers for other people as a family tradition. She questioned, "Does anybody have any prayer requests before I pray?"

Marva spoke, "Pray for Robert to give his life to the Lord."

Mary Ellen looked up and Mama Mae questioned, "Little Stockings, you got something for me to pray about?"

"No ma'am. Yes."

"Well which is it?"

They laughed with the exception of Mama Mae and Mary Ellen.

"Say a prayer for Nathan. He needs to be saved."

Everyone nodded 'yes.'

Mama Mae had concluded her prayer. Mary Ellen adored Miss Beatrice's griddlecakes as she spoke between bites, "Mama, what do you think about me moving to Ohio to teach at Oldwood College?"

Everyone stopped eating and looked at her. Mae interrupted before Mama Mae had a chance to think about how she would feel if Mary Ellen was to permanently relocate. "What about your life here?" Her brows arched.

Mama Mae cleared her throat and spoke while she rubbed the sides of her mouth, "What brought all of this on? I thought for sure that Nate was interested in you. I mean after that Trotter boy left, he hung around."

Mary Ellen swallowed her food and then drank a sip of juice. She glanced at Mama Mae. "Now that God has blessed me to finish college, it would make sense for me to apply my education to something worthwhile. You know something that can benefit others. I mean that I didn't obtain my doctorate to sit around Beauford Place all day doing nothing."

She glanced at Jack and noticed that her comment caused him to feel uneasy. Marva shamefully lowered her head at the comment. Mama Mae played with her food with her fork and commented, "You're not Little Stockings anymore. You're a full grown woman and if that's what you feel is best then do it."

Guilt filled Mary Ellen's heart while she looked around the table at them. She tried to sway everyone including herself. "I feel that I need to give something back. I've been blessed and now it's time for me to bless others."

This time she peered at Mr. John who nodded his head sideways.

Marva pleaded with her facial expression along with her voice as she placed her fork beside her plate, "Can't you teach around here? There are lots of people that can benefit from you right here in Tradassa Town!"

Mae concurred, "Amen, ain't that the truth?"

Mr. John looked at Mary Ellen and spoke as she wished that she had never sat across from him. "Little Stockings if you feel that fleeing to Ohio best suits you, I suppose that's what you should do. I just hope you don't get there and find out that it's not all what you expected and end up disappointed."

This is one time that Mary Ellen had hoped that Mr. John would've kept his wisdom to himself. Mama Mae stopped eating and placed her hands on her lap after blotting her mouth with a napkin. She looked at Mary Ellen and asked, "How long do you plan to stay up there? I mean is this a permanent move?"

"I don't—."

Of all the people that chose to express themselves, Jack finally addressed the situation. "From what I understand, you have to make some type of commitment like sign a contract for so many years." He sat straight up and looked at Mary Ellen with his narrow deep-set eyes.

Mary Ellen's eyes widened along with the others as they were focused on Jack. They realized for the first time that Jack wasn't ignorant. He just wasn't much of a conversationalist.

A frown unfolded on Mr. John's face when he looked at Mary Ellen. He clasped his hands and thumped his thumbs together, which was a greater annoyance that exceeded the others as they offered their commentary.

Mary Ellen became extremely frustrated and wanted to end the discussion. Therefore, she chose to end it her way. There was firmness in her demeanor as she spoke resolutely, "I appreciate all your concern and input. But I've made my decision and that's all there is to say. Mama, I'll be sure to let you know in plenty of time before I choose to leave."

Mama Mae replied, "Alright, you know what's best," as she released a sigh and repositioned her body in the chair. She muttered, "You've only been back here a few days and now you want to leave again." She didn't finish her breakfast.

The others had solemn expressions with the exception of Jack and Mr. John. Mr. John silently reproved Mary Ellen's decision by making eye contact with her.

Mary Ellen had convinced herself that she was doing the right thing—running away that is.

Chapter Eight

Mary Ellen stroked the keys of the upright piano as she found herself overcome with boredom and frustration. She played a song from the hymnal book, which Mama Mae was fond of titled *My Eyes Are on the Lord* and sang with vivacity.

The formal parlor living room was beautiful with oversized oil paintings adorned with fancy cartouches, ornately carved wooden chairs upholstered with costly fabric, and a lovely carved wooden high mantle with a fireplace accented with marble. The oversized picturesque windows were embellished with fine drapery, tiebacks, and sheer curtains that permitted just the right amount of sunlight to enter the room. The room housed a long mahogany bookcase filled with Bibles, poetry books, and other books on literature. Victorian lamps covered with lavish shades matched the furnishings and drapery. The room had a tray ceiling edged with ornate crown molding craftsmanship. A large crystal chandelier hung from the center of the ceiling. There was a wine-colored Victorian style davenport with matching chairs positioned on the opposite side of the parlor alongside a few fine art marble sculptures.

When she was a small girl, her parents would sit her on the piano bench and allow her to play. Little Mary Ellen would grin as if she knew what she was doing. Benjamin noticed her keen interest and paid wages to a local piano teacher to instruct her. Sometimes, they would stand her atop a small table for her to sing hymnals.

Everyone believed that someday she would sing gospel songs on a professional level and earn a fulltime living. Nonetheless, Mary Ellen's fondness has always been her penmanship. She loved to write and never seemed to get enough of it. That's one of the reasons that she never sang in the church choir.

It didn't seem to matter what she did to distract herself from focusing on her decision and Nathan because nothing seemed to work. Mary Ellen knew in her heart what to do when faced with a tough situation that proved to work each time. She was resilient to fasting because she hated denying her flesh. Nevertheless, she knew that this called for fasting and prayer without the influence of family members and her selfishness. Mary Ellen realized that this was a time to focus on her relationship with the Lord and seek His guidance. She told herself that this was the right direction to take—fasting and praying as there had been numerous distractions that brought about confusion. And God is not the author of confusion but of love and peace. She realized that her family meant well in their own unique way and that she too hoped that her decision was for the good of everyone. However, she needed to be sure as there remained in her an air of uncertainty that didn't feel quite right. She didn't want to go in a direction that would permanently alter her life resulting in negative consequences. She desired the blessing of God upon her life. She knew that would give her the peace that she had been missing since her return to Beauford Place.

Her father's biblical teachings and wisdom returned to her. He used to explain that when you don't know what to do and you're uncertain about a decision, take time to fast, pray, and seek the wisdom of God. She usually preferred to begin her fast in the morning as she would anoint herself and pray.

Mary Ellen walked over to a chair that had a table positioned beside it. A large voluminous white Bible sat atop the table open-faced with pages edged in gold. She sat down, rested her head against her propped arm, silently read some passages of Scriptures, and meditated on them.

Peace I leave with you, my peace I give unto you: not as the world giveth, give I unto you. Let not your heart be troubled, neither let it be afraid. John 14:27

And hope maketh not ashamed; because the love of God is shed abroad in our hearts by the Holy Ghost which is given unto us. Romans 5:5

And we know that all things work together for good to them that love God, to them who are the called according to his purpose. Romans 8:28

But God commendeth his love toward us, in that, while we were yet sinners, Christ died for us. Romans 5:8

Let him know, that he which converteth the sinner from the error of his way shall save a soul from death, and shall hide a multitude of sins. James 5:20

After Mary Ellen read the Scriptures, her attention was drawn to the latter one—*James 5:20,* which she reread audibly and meditated on for approximately twenty minutes. Afterwards, she knelt in front of the chair, prayed for guidance, for God to touch Nathan's heart, and not allow any harm to come to him. About the space of a half-hour had passed then she stood, proceeded to the bookshelf, grabbed her father's breviary, and silently read some of the prayers.

Mary Ellen didn't want to sit on the front verandah as she often loved to do so. Instead, she chose to take a long stroll back to the small wooden bridge. She observed Nathan as he tended to the horses. He had been singing his heart out and smiled when he saw her. Mary Ellen casually waved, as she didn't want to stop and talk albeit she desired to ride Rain to revisit the meadow.

Nathan watched her until she disappeared from his vision. He told himself that he wouldn't follow her as he resumed his duties and that she was just a friend and their relationship couldn't go any farther. He knew that he was lying to himself. He convinced himself that she wasn't concerned about him and that he wouldn't be there much longer because it was for the best.

Mary Ellen's walk seemed to journey endlessly, as it was different without a horse. Finally, she was happy to see the small bridge and the meadow with the field of wildflowers that she adored. She had desired to prolong her visit there earlier, which was the reason that she returned. It was a pleasant place to unwind and get a break from the distractions. She understood why Nathan liked the meadow.

Mary Ellen gathered a few wildflowers, stood on the bridge, and leaned against the railing. She turned around and noticed the wildflowers floating in the water that she had tossed in earlier that morning.

No—she told herself that she wouldn't think about Nathan. She didn't look forward to fasting either. Nevertheless, she knew that it would benefit her spiritually. She saw her reflection in the water and chuckled. She loosened her hair, fluffed it wild, and peered at her reflection again as she chuckled a second time. She told herself that she wasn't anyone's sweetheart—least of all—Nathan's.

Mary Ellen plucked petals from some of the wildflowers, tossed them in the water, and watched them float. It startled to sprinkle as a few drops splashed the outer part of her hands. She told herself that it was just a shower because the sun was still shining. When a cool zephyr blew her hair about her face it betokened a coming storm as a large dark cloud approached from the north. She was unaware because her eyes were closed as she leaned back and drew a deep breath while her hair blew about. She lifted her hands and released the wildflowers as they fell to the bridge and toppled in the water.

Mary Ellen felt another rain shower that she hoped would go away like the former one. Suddenly a torrent of rain poured and became heavy to the point that she could barely move or see. She was drenched. Her hair covered her face and she mopped it away from her eyes. The rain was in her eyes as she batted her long lashes. "Oh no!" she hollered.

She had a long way to walk back. She tried to ease herself off the bridge and stepped into muddy ground that seemed to grip her legs. Mary Ellen was a mess as she slowly trudged through the mud. At one point, she lost one of her shoes as she lifted her leg from the mud and fell over. Her hands dug into the mud and her knees sank. Her dress and undergarments were mud-soaked. Her foot slipped from her other shoe as it was stuck in the mud. She sobbed hard as her voice resonated strongly from within.

Mary Ellen felt something tug at her and she became frightened. She stood on her knees, looked up, and saw that it was Nathan. She was glad to see him!

"Help me! I'm stuck!"

He yelled, "Grab hold of my arm—hurry!"

He pulled her up as she mounted Midnight and he yelled, "Yaw!"

Midnight quickly rode away. The rain had started to slack after they rode out from underneath the dark storm cloud. She gripped his waist as she trembled from being wet with the cold wind blowing about. Midnight seemed to know exactly where to go.

The rain had ceased by the time they arrived at their destination. Nathan rode directly to the rear verandah. He dismounted, assisted Mary Ellen from the steed, and carried her up the steps. Mr. John, Mr. Pope, Miss Beatrice, and Miss Edna were in the kitchen. Mr. John opened the door for Nathan to carry her inside the mudroom. She was a mess.

Miss Beatrice hollered, "There she is!"

Mr. John spoke, "Everybody was wondering where she was 'cause a storm's approaching." He pulled up a chair. "Sit her down here."

Nathan gently placed her on the chair.

Miss Edna ran to the parlor and informed Mama Mae. Afterwards, she quickly grabbed some towels and returned to the mudroom. Nathan grabbed one of the towels, kneeled, blotted her face, and brushed her hair back with his hand.

He questioned her in front of everyone teasingly in a low tone, "What are you going to do without me?"

Her lips trembled from being cold as she tried to speak, "I—I don't know." She gave a slight smile as her lips trembled. He spoke, "You need to get inside and get out of those wet clothes and take a nice hot bath."

Miss Beatrice spoke, "I put some water on for tea."

Nathan was soaked but he didn't seem cold. He had become accustomed to working outside in stormy weather conditions.

Mama Mae stepped in the doorway of the mudroom. "What happened to Little Stockings? Child you are a mess!"

Nathan stood and explained, "Well ma'am she got caught in the heavy storm. She walked to the old bridge by herself. And when I saw the sky getting dark back there, that's when I rode out to look for her and I brought her back here."

Miss Edna spoke, "I drew some bath water for you Little Stockings. It should be ready soon."

Mary Ellen still shivered as she barely spoke, "Thanks."

She looked up at Nathan and beckoned him to come closer. He kneeled to hear what she had to say as he peered into her eyes. Mary Ellen admired his deep dark eyes. She spoke as her lips trembled, "Thanks for coming to get me."

He responded, "Anytime—Mary Ellen."

Everyone looked at Nathan when he addressed her as Mary Ellen instead of Little Stockings. He prepared to stand and she tugged on his sleeve. He stooped and peered in her eyes again. "What is it?"

"I—I'd like to invite you for supper tonight; that is if it's alright with you."

His eyes lit up and he smiled, "I'll come back after I get cleaned up."

He stood, excused himself, and departed.

Mary Ellen stood in front of her vanity and held a dress against her to determine whether she wanted to wear it. She didn't know what to make of the event from today as she told herself that this was the second time Nathan came to her rescue. She told herself that the Lord must be trying to show her something. She questioned her integrity. If Nathan can come to her rescue, why couldn't she come to his?

Nathan had spruced himself up and sat in his comfortable chair just before he prepared to walk across to the mansion. He pondered over the recent turn of events. He told himself that he wasn't sure of what he was doing. Nevertheless, he knew that he was in love with her.

Mary Ellen sat behind the large desk in the study. She retrieved a fountain pen and then glanced at the typewriter that formerly belonged to her father. She returned the pen to its proper place, inserted a sheet of paper into the typewriter, and paused for a few minutes before typing, as she appeared to be in deep thought. A soft smile emerged as she slowly typed a new poem inspired by the afternoon event. Afterwards, she released the paper from the typewriter, proceeded to the parlor to wait for Nathan, and was surprised upon entering the room to see him sitting in an upholstered chair. He immediately stood and waited for her to sit. She sat on the davenport facing him. Mary Ellen was adorned in a wine-colored floor-length dress with short bouffant elastic sewn sleeves trimmed with lace. She wore a pearl necklace and matching earrings. Her hair was in a long thick crinkly rope braid that hung down her back.

Nathan was clad in black dressy trousers with a matching white split-band collar shirt and a black western bowtie. He wore a red weskit with gold appliqués with a gold pocket watch. His sleeves were cuff-linked in gold with his initials N.J.H. He still maintained his dark crinkly hair neatly trimmed close with a slight wave pattern and parted on the left side. He was freshly shaven and Mary Ellen could smell his cologne as she purposely drew a deep breath. He wore ankle-length black and white spat boots. He looked handsome sitting there with the slight cleft in his chin.

He eyed the paper in her hands. "Did you write another poem?"

She laughed. "How did you know?"

He pointed his finger at the paper that she was holding.

"Oh."

He looked at her and slightly raised his brows. Mary Ellen stared at his brows, as they were nice and complemented his face. "Well, aren't you going to read it or would you rather sit on the verandah and read it?"

She smiled. "It is nice and cool out there and supper's not ready yet. I just hope we don't get wet again. And speaking of wet, we better make certain that where we sit isn't wet."

He chuckled as he stood, "I guess I'll just have to rescue you all over again."

He reached for his black soft gambler-style hat that was perched on the hall tree stand and then held the door as she proceeded to the front verandah. She ran her hand across the swing and sat down and he checked the chair on the left side opposite to her father's former favorite chair. He sat down and spoke, "I don't think the storm made it this way yet."

"If it did, Miss Edna must've wiped the furniture out here." They glanced upward and discerned the clouds. She cleared her throat and began, "This is titled *Rainfall*."

They laughed and he said, "It's befitting."

"I watch the rain as it falls from the sky,
As a fount from heaven way upon high.
I cannot help but wonder if the rain that pours,
Are tears from God overflowing through heaven's doors.
Then comes the arched bow displaying its many colors,
Reminiscent of Your promise to myself as well as others.
You nourish and replenish the green grass of many lands,
And with love You outstretched the palms of Your hands.
The vastness of Your wonders causes me to be in mirth,
And to hear You say I love you O' inhabitants of the earth."

He looked at her intensely. "How do you come up with these inspiring poems? Did you learn this in college?"

She gave a slight closed-mouthed smile. "I was blessed by God to write like this for many years. I attended college because I desire to teach others to better themselves."

He spoke in admiration, "You probably earned good grades when you attended college and possibly all the way through school."

She smiled.

"How did they feel about your poetry in college?" His eyes remained focused on hers.—

She admired his sincere openness. "They liked my poetry. In fact, one of my poems was published by Oldwood College."

"I'm impressed."

He leaned back comfortably on the chair.

"Let me ask you something, if you desire to teach others to better themselves, then why don't you help some of the less fortunate?"

Her brows tightened slightly. "I never thought about teaching the less fortunate."

He pursed his lips for a second. "It was just a thought because people that are attending college are already improving themselves."

She gave him a straightforward look as she changed the subject. "I'd like to thank you for rescuing me again. You've seen me at my best and you've seen me at my worse."

He gave a closed-mouth smile and tilted his head slightly as he leaned his head against his propped arm. He remained focused on her. "Even at your worse, you're still a very beautiful woman."

"Thank you." Mary Ellen replied calmly. She has received compliments from many possible suitors. But there was something about his compliments that made her feel wonderful as it showed in her eyes and countenance. She told herself that she wasn't going to bother him concerning his vengeful plans as she had placed everything in God's hands. Mary Ellen knows that she can't change his heart—only God can.

"Wait right here." She went inside upstairs to her bedroom. She returned outside momentarily and handed him a framed photograph of her. Mary Ellen noticed a gleam that appeared in his eyes when he looked at the photograph. Afterwards, he resumed looking at her as she stood in front of him.

"Are you just showing this to me or do I get to keep it?"

"It's yours if you'd like to keep it." She tapped the glass on the frame with her fingernail. "I had this taken when I was in college."

It was a lovely black and white photograph of her wearing a long-flowing satin evening gown embellished with sequins that resembled a wedding gown. She wore long white gloves and jewelry that accentuated the gown. Her long hair had been pressed and styled in a bouffant coiffure adorned with decorative combs. Ringlets of curls cascaded downward that enhanced the overall affect.

"Thanks." His face lit up like a schoolboy that had just received a love note from a girl that he had a crush on.

He placed the photograph to his lips and gave it a quick kiss. She chuckled and then resumed her seated position.

He glanced at her. "I guess I have to kiss your picture since I can't kiss you anymore."

She placed her hand over her mouth and laughed again that caused her abdomen to bounce rhythmically. Nathan didn't notice her full reaction because he still clutched the photograph and studied every detail.

Afterwards, he studied her as she sat positioned comfortably on the swing. She twitched a bit as she responded with an uneasy reaction upon noticing him watching her.

He carefully placed the photograph facing upward on the ledge of the verandah, clasped his hands, leaned forward, and then addressed her candidly. "So tell me my new found friend, how do friends conduct themselves properly or what you consider to be proper since we're only friends?"

She hesitated to answer and told herself again that she wouldn't bring up the subject of his parents nor his vengeful quest. Strong breathing emanated from her as she tried to remain calm.

Mary Ellen nervously gestured with her right hand during her response. "I believe that friends are people that discuss things of a personal nature—things they wouldn't normally share with anyone else. You know—confide in one another, share their opinions and views, laugh together, cry together I suppose."

He looked at her with straightforwardness. "Humph."

Her brows rose slightly as she shrugged her shoulders and lifted her hands. "What's the problem now? You asked me a question and I gave you my opinion."

Surprisingly, he stood and she looked inquisitively as he positioned himself next to her on the swing. He placed his arm around her and she wrung her hands then sighed.

"Nathan what are you doing? You have a persistent nature."

He looked sternly into her eyes. "Nothing. I just wanted to sit next to you."

"You like to play games, don't you?"

"Hardly. I've shared things about me to you that I never told anyone except your father."

Her lashes fluttered as she drew a deep breath and placed her hand over his. She promised herself repeatedly that she wouldn't succumb to her emotions. Therefore, she withdrew her hand from his.

Courageously she peered deep into his eyes and straightened her posture. "Are you still contemplating carrying out your mission that you spoke about the other day?"

He tousled her braid between his fingers. "If you mean avenging my folks, the answer is no." Mary Ellen's eyes lit up with joy before he finished what he had to say.

"I'm not contemplating; I intend to fully execute my mission."

She became expressionless. "This plan that you've contrived will be your demise. You've become your own nemesis—not the men that murdered your parents."

He developed a solemn expression as his eyes lowered.

She emitted a sigh. "You probably don't understand the words that I just used."

He tilted his head at her and smirked, "Humph. I'll have you to know that although I didn't attend college; my father did his utmost to see that I attended school and earn good grades. And he gave me a dictionary and made me learn the definitions and spellings of words everyday!"

He had taken her by surprise.

"He also made me write sentences everyday using the words that I learned!"

Mary Ellen became offensive as her nostrils flared slightly when she drew a deep breath. "Nathan, you don't have to be so curt." She swallowed. "I don't think that you realize that if you carry out this mission, that it not only affects you, but it affects me too. I could be considered an accessory." She stopped as her eyes became glassy and drew a deep breath.

He relaxed his countenance and spoke contritely. "I'm sorry. I hadn't realized. We shouldn't discuss this anymore."

She clutched his hand taut, which drew his attention. "I don't think that you understand the impact you've made on me and you want to go and destroy your life—for what?"

He placed his other hand atop Mary Ellen's and repositioned his body to fully face her. "I didn't think that I had any type of impact on you because you don't seem to act as if I do."

Her eyes saddened at she looked upon him and tried to constrain the deep breathing that emanated from within. "Nathan, I love you. And if that isn't enough for you, I don't know what else to say."

His eyes lit up and he released his hand from hers and swept aside a tendril of hair from her face. He lifted her chin and kissed her sweetly as she wrapped her arms around his strong shoulders. Afterwards, he held her in his arms and she whispered, "You always seem to come to my rescue. You need to be rescued from yourself."

Their embrace ended as he calmly spoke, "I love you."

She fought back the tears and sniffed. "I don't know what to do except pray. I want to teach. You want to kill. I'm saved and you're not. This relationship is a disaster and a rockslide."

He stroked her hand and kissed her forehead.

She continued, "What type of future could we possibly have—me visiting you in prison or perhaps placing flowers on your grave?"

Nathan's brows tightened. "Are you saying that you'd be interested in having a future with me—a cowboy? I thought that you wanted to leave this place."

She entreated him with her eyes, "The only reason that I desire to leave is because there's no reason for me to stay. There's nothing holding me here."

He repositioned his body forward on the swing, leaned his elbows on his knees, and rested his chin in his hands.

"But what about you wanting to become a teacher?"

"I'd like to teach. I just don't want to sit around here all day and do nothing like the rest of my family."

He looked at her. "I can understand that. I'd rather work on the ranch than do what Jack does."

She smirked, "What does Jack do?"

"Nothing." They chuckled and he gave her hand a gentle squeeze.

He peered into her eyes and spoke. "How could I provide for you? Would you be happy marrying a man like me?"

She didn't answer.

"If my folks hadn't been murdered, I would've gone to college and became a minister and I would've been the type of man that's suitable for a woman of your caliber because that's what you deserve."

Mary Ellen looked as if she was analyzing everything that he had spoken. "When I see you working, you seem happy with what you do and you're always singing and when I wake up in the morning I hear you singing."

He smiled. "That's because I love to sing and I love working with horses—cattle too."

"Do you feel degraded doing what you love?"

He paused a moment then responded, "No." He patted her hand. "You probably won't believe this but I used to enjoy reading the Bible and attending church too. It was one of my favorite things to do."

"Why don't you give it a try again because the only reason that you stopped is because of what happened to your parents."

He looked hurt. "I think about it sometimes. I still have my father's Bible. I haven't really prayed since it happened. I just couldn't bear to pray—can't seem to get the words out." His eyes watered. "Mary Ellen, I'm so tired of crying. I'm so tired." He released a sigh that seemed to help him relax as he lowered his head.

She gave his back a gentle pat and rub as he fought back the tears. "I feel that somehow God has abandoned me and He wouldn't be interested in hearing from me at this point in my life."

Mary Ellen interlocked her fingers with his and entreated him emphatically, "I don't know how you figured that the Lord would abandon you. Jesus loves you Nathan and you need to realize that. Would you mind if I prayed for you so that He can come to your rescue the way you've come to mine? You need to give this to the Lord and allow Him to fight your battles."

He nodded 'yes' then spoke, "I need you to pray for me every time you think about me."

She looked sincere, "Well I'm thinking about you now so let's pray."

He closed his eyes and bowed his head. Mary Ellen prayed very hard as she trembled during prayer and a spirit of peace overshadowed them. Afterwards, they rocked on the swing for a while with their hands still interlocked. Nathan's countenance changed, as he was more relaxed than he had been in a long time. Mary Ellen knew that the Lord was working already. She told herself that God works in mysterious ways and that all things work together for the good of them that love God from the passage that she read earlier.

Miss Edna opened the door and announced, "Supper's ready." Mary Ellen noticed that Miss Edna had changed into another uniform. The one that she wore earlier had gotten soiled from assisting Mary Ellen out of her mud-soaked clothing.

Nathan stood and extended his hand to assist Mary Ellen up from the swing. He proceeded to the ledge and grabbed the framed photograph.

Mary Ellen asked Nathan, "Are you hungry?"

He chuckled, "Yes ma'am and it smells good in there." He extended his arm to her. She wrapped her arm around his and they proceeded inside.

Chapter Nine

All eyes were upon them as Nathan escorted Mary Ellen in the dining room. He seated her with his gentleman mannerism. Miss Edna had the table set beautifully. Mr. John joined them for supper. As usual, Mr. Pope planned to dine in the kitchen with Miss Edna and Miss Beatrice. Mae strategically positioned herself beside Nathan for observational reasons with Jack on the opposite side of her. Mary Ellen sat on the opposite side of Nathan. Mr. John sat directly across from Nathan because he desired to do so. Marva sat on the left side of Mr. John. Mary Ellen told herself that it was going to be an interesting supper.

Mama Mae smiled at Nathan as she was seated on the right side of Mr. John. "It's good to have you join us again. You up for blessing the food?" Everyone was accustomed to Mama Mae's solecisms.

"I'll do the best I can." Nathan glanced at Mary Ellen who became uneasy. Mae leaned back in her seat with a stupefied expression and looked upon Nathan.

Nathan began, *"Let us bow our heads in reverence to the Lord. Lord, bless this food we're prepared to receive. Bless this fellowship and bless the hands that prepared the meal as we offer thanksgiving and praise to You. Amen."*

Everyone followed in unison, *"Amen."*

Mary Ellen whispered, "You did well."

"Thank you."

Large platters circulated the table that consisted of sirloin steak with onions and gravy, mashed potatoes, and string beans. Everyone dropped a bolus of mashed potatoes on their plate and heaped Miss Beatrice's mouth-watering gravy atop. The string bean platter was next in circulation.

Mama Mae's brows hunched when she eyed the string beans. She spoke in her usual loud southerly tone, "Miss Beatrice, what's wrong with these string beans here?"

Everyone paused and looked at Miss Beatrice who calmly replied with her deep southern voice, "There's nothing at all wrong with those string beans—they came out of a can."

Mae rolled her eyes and smirked—of course without Mama Mae's awareness.

Mama Mae responded, "I likes mine fresh. I could look at these and tell they weren't fresh."

Nathan chuckled and Miss Beatrice nonchalantly returned to the kitchen. The steak platter was being circulated. Mary Ellen jabbed through the steaks until she was able to find a small piece. Nathan chuckled again as he watched her place the tiny piece of meat on her plate.

Mr. John commented, "That piece ain't big enough to feed a starving jackrabbit."

Everyone laughed including Mary Ellen.

Mama Mae got started. "Little Stockings eats just enough to feed a bird. That child needs some meat on those bones."

Mary Ellen blurted, "Perhaps if I gained weight, you'd all stop calling me Little Stockings!"

Marva added as she sucked on a bone, "Don't do that, they might start calling you Big Stockings like me!"

Mr. John jumped in, "No we can't have two Big Stockings under one roof. We'd have to come up with something else."

Nathan was beside himself as everyone burst into laughter. Surprisingly, he commented. "I think she's fine just the way she is. I like a small woman. They're easier to lift."

Mr. John added, "You ought to know. The way you carried her in here today; she looked like a muddy sow."

Everyone laughed hilariously and Mary Ellen's eyes enlarged with her lips slightly parted. A bout of laughter emanated from the kitchen as the staff heard Mr. John's comment.

Nathan chuckled and retorted, "That's enough. Don't talk about my sweetheart."

Mae looked at Nathan and snapped her finger. "Ooh, I knew it! I knew it! I knew it!"

Mama Mae spoke up as she fished through the string beans with her fork that she detested, "Hush up child. That ain't none of your business."

Miss Beatrice entered the room carrying a large triple-layered frosted peach cake that probably would've won first prize at the county fair.

Marva commented, "Miss Beatrice that looks good."

Mr. John added, "Miss Beatrice, you sure do wonders with those peaches."

Mae jumped in again, as she frowned, "It's better than what some people do with peaches like make peach liquor."

Nathan laughed again. Miss Beatrice smiled sheepishly and returned to the kitchen to dine.

Mary Ellen looked at Nathan. "Please excuse my family. You've eaten here before and you know how they can be."

Nathan calmly replied, "They don't bother me." He continued to enjoy his meal as he shoved a forkful of string beans in his mouth.

She was relieved that he could handle them.

Mr. John studied Nathan and Mary Ellen. "So are you two finally courtin' now?"

Nathan responded as he glanced at Mary Ellen, "That's up to the lady."

Mr. John inquired again between bites of steak, "Didn't I see that tall lanky fella over here the other day?" He rocked his fork with a small piece of steak attached to it while he awaited a response. Nathan and Mary Ellen didn't respond. Mae and Marva's brows arched as they glanced at Mary Ellen and then at Nathan.

Mama Mae calmly blotted her mouth with a cloth napkin and responded. "If you mean that Trotter boy—he dropped by."

Mae prepared to insert her fork in her mouth after she speared a piece of steak and hesitated as she looked at Nathan and then Mama Mae. "Did I miss something new?" Her focus shifted toward Mary Ellen. Nathan remained calm.

Jack interrupted before anyone could respond, "Big Mae, that's enough! Finish your supper and let them be."

Everyone looked at Jack and marveled. This was the second time he said something that made a heap of sense.

Nathan rubbed Mary Ellen's hand and spoke softly as he looked at her, "I'm glad you didn't choose Lawrence."

Mary Ellen stopped eating and looked at Nathan. "I'm glad I didn't either."

Mary Ellen passed on the peach cake. Nathan helped himself to a hefty piece. Mary Ellen took a fork and tasted some from his saucer. Miss Beatrice had done it again! The cake was fabulous and everyone enjoyed it.

After supper ended Nathan and Mary Ellen excused themselves and he thanked everyone for having him over. When Mary Ellen walked Nathan to the door after supper, he grabbed his hat and the photograph of her from the hall tree stand on his way out to the verandah.

As they stood on the verandah, they noticed a beautiful rainbow arched in the sky. Nathan smiled as he admired it. "Just like your poem."

He turned around and looked at Mary Ellen then kissed her forehead. "I'd better go. It's late for me and I have an early day tomorrow. And I'm tired."

Mary Ellen smiled. "You always have an early day. Remember, I can hear your singing."

She looked in his eyes. "You look exhausted; probably from lifting me up from the mud." She smiled.

"You're not a heavy woman and you definitely don't remind me of a sow. You're beautiful Mary Ellen and you're very special to me." His eyes looked glassy and weary. "I don't think I could ever forget you—never in life."

He stroked her cheek as her eyes watered and spoke, "Good night."

She watched him stride in the direction of the carriage house. Afterwards, she returned inside and ascended upstairs to her room while clutching the sides of her dress.

Nathan entered his dwelling, sat down on his davenport, and removed his spats. He got up, retrieved the crumpled piece of paper from the waste can, and did his best to flatten his initial attempt at writing poetry. He retrieved his notepad and fountain pen and bowdlerized the writings from the crumpled piece of paper until he had finally written something that pleased him.

My Plea My Love
The gentle caress of your hands upon mine,
Bring comfort and sooth my troubled mind.
Brokenness has wearied my young tired soul,
Tell me my love what direction should I go?

Your heart of love captured me unaware,
Blessed by knowing that you truly care.
Your patience and understanding is what I need,
And prayer not to commit this horrible misdeed.

I stand in need of a complete mind renewal,
Can you help me my lovely sparkling jewel?
Vexation and frustration has grappled me tight,
Will God deliver me from my terrible plight?

After Nathan penned his poem, he told himself that
it sounded more like a plea for help. He seemed to pour
his heart out on paper. He asked himself whether the Lord
really did still care about him and whether he could forgive
those men and whether he could be forgiven. He told
himself that he wasn't sure what he would do if he was face-
to-face with the murderers. He questioned himself as to

whether he would be able to walk away and go on with his life and would he ever truly be happy and fulfilled again?

He reminded himself that Mary Ellen told him that she loved him. A gentle smile emerged on his face as he prepared himself for bed. Nathan was finally able to enjoy a peaceful night's rest.

Mary Ellen opened the double-doors leading to her verandah, stepped out, and talked to God audibly. "Lord thank You for blessing me this day. I see Your hand moving in this situation. I don't quite understand any of this. But I know that You're with me and that You understand. Bless Nathan to turn his life over to You. Bless him not to go after those men. Lord I'm asking You to soften his heart and give him a heart of love, compassion, and forgiveness. Bless him to be at peace concerning his parents. Bless him to know that You have them in Your hands and that they rest with You."

She looked at the sky and drew a deep breath. Afterwards, she returned inside to her room and climbed into bed as she too was tired from the events of the day.

She draped the covers around her and stared at the stars in the sky until she finally drifted off to sleep.

Mary Ellen had awakened very early as she had gone to bed earlier than usual. She freshened herself and dressed in a lovely floor-length laced-bodice dress with matching laced shoes. Her pastel purplish dress was made from cottony fabric with satiny ribbons laced throughout the bouffant sleeves. She's quite fond of pastels. Mary Ellen sat at her vanity and pulled her thick hair back in a bun. She inserted decorative combs around the bun. She examined her coiffure in the looking-glass and was satisfied with her appearance.

This was the day she had chosen to begin her consecration. She removed a tiny vial from her vanity drawer that contained anointing oil. She placed a small blot on her forehead then returned the vial to the drawer. She knelt beside her bed and petitioned the Lord for her requests. She promised herself that she would pray unselfishly. She began her dirge and prayed strongly for Nathan and others as God would see that her needs were met. She prayed for a half-hour and then wiped the blot of oil from her forehead.

Her timing was impeccable, as Nathan had just started his morning crooning only seconds after she concluded her prayer petition. She slowly eased herself from the floor to prevent tripping over her long dress and made her way to the verandah just outside of her bedroom. She looked down and grinned at Nathan who was perched on Midnight as he played his guitar. He sang, "Mary Ellen, Mary Ellen, I'm captured by your love. Mary Ellen, Mary Ellen, sent from heaven above."

She laughed until her eyes watered as she clutched the railing. Nathan displayed no shame in his crooning. He certainly wasn't the bashful type. It was difficult to provoke him to embarrassment because he isn't the type of man that's easily embarrassed. He's outspoken, yet mannerly, and deeply in love; albeit he does have some rough edges that require smoothing.

He beckoned with his arm for her to come down. She returned inside and made her descent on the stairs while carefully clutching the sides of her dress. When she stepped outside to the verandah, she was taken aback to see that Nathan had arrived and stood on the steps. He smiled and lifted his cowboy hat. "Morning."

He was dressed in his black cowboy attire that he wore the day they met.

Mary Ellen smiled with a mixture of a chuckle as she stood with her arms folded. "Good morning. You look well rested."

"I slept pretty good last night. I needed the rest." His eyes twinkled. "You look beautiful and your hair looks nice like that."

She chuckled at his compliment as she patted her hair. Before she could seat herself, he reached inside a compartment sewn inside his black leather weskit and retrieved the poem that he had written.

She asked in bewilderment, "What's that?" Her lips parted.

Nathan sat in her father's former favorite chair and placed his hat on the ledge. "I wrote something for you to read." He leaned over and handed it to her.

Mary Ellen glanced at it and a look of disbelief appeared on her face. She spoke slowly in doubt. "You didn't write this!" She handed it back to him.

He was taken aback. "I wrote this when I left you last night. It took me a while. But I finally got it done. Now read it!" He tried to give it back to her and she refused to accept it.

She countered, "You recite it! I always recite mine to you. Now it's your turn."

He smiled. "But your voice sounds sweet when you recite poetry. Mine will sound rough."

She replied smiling, "I like your voice and it's supposed to sound *rough* as you call it. I prefer to call it manly. I know this much, you sing beautifully. You can serenade me anytime although it's usually done at night."

She told herself, now I really know why Big Stockings enjoys his singing. He has a nice voice.

"Then I'll have to serenade you some night."

He recited the poem to her. When he finished her eyes were filled with tears. He hadn't anticipated her reaction and was stunned when he looked at her.

"I was hoping that you'd be happy. I didn't mean to make you cry." He removed his neckerchief and blotted her eyes.

She touched his hand and explained, "I'm not sad. I'm happy and amazed. I didn't think that you had it in you. And then again, you're always crooning songs in the morning."

He chuckled and slightly reared his head back. "I like to sing when I work and sometimes when I'm not working. It helps to take my mind off things that trouble me."

He handed her the poem. "I wrote this for you and I'd like you to keep it in case—." He stopped.

She looked at him and spoke softly, "Nothing's going to happen to you Nathan. You may not understand or believe what I'm saying right now. But I have faith in God that everything's going to turn out alright."

He was enlightened by her words of faith.

She developed a look of ambiguity. "Tell me something, do you think that my family is crazy? You know the way they act at the supper table?"

He laughed as his eyes squinted. "Why would you ask me a question like that?"

"I just wanted to know should you decide to fully commit to this relationship some day."

He looked serene and leaned forward. "I'm still wrestling with some issues. But know this; my heart is yours if you'll have it. Just keep praying for me. Every time you think of me, pray for me."

She nodded, "I understand and I'm keeping your name before God."

He gave her hands a gentle squeeze and kissed them. He prepared to stand. "I'd better get back to work."

Before he was able to stand, she grabbed his arm. "Nathan, I must tell you that I'm going to be distant from you because I'm consecrating myself in prayer. So you probably won't see me for several days, unless of course you drive me to church on Sundays. And if you do, I still want to be distant until I'm finished."

He fully understood from his upbringing in the church. "I'll miss seeing you."

She held his hand and proceeded to explain, "It doesn't—."

He interrupted, "You don't have to explain. I know what that means. Remember, I was raised in the church. I'll see you after you're finished."

He descended the steps, walked a few paces, pivoted, and spoke, "I love you Mary Ellen and remember me in your prayers," then blew her a kiss.

Mary Ellen shut herself away from everyone. She began her prayer and devotion. Although her flesh detested being denied, she remained steadfast in seeking the face of God.

As the days passed, she became spiritually keen and strong. Her spirit was refreshed and her mind was renewed. Her spirit was tuned into the Spirit of God.

Mary Ellen gained confidence in knowing that God had given her the strength to endure the trial that she was faced with. She gained newfound trust in God that He was with her. She placed Nathan in God's hands to change his heart. She meditated on several passages of Scriptures. One in particular was, *The king's heart is in the hand of the LORD, as the rivers of water: he turneth it whithersoever he will. Proverbs 21:1*

Chapter Ten

Mary Ellen was up and about as her days of consecration had come to a close. She missed seeing Nathan. Mr. Pope had replaced Nathan as their Sunday driver. Nathan had decided against driving Mary Ellen to church on Sundays because he didn't want to be a distraction to her.

Mary Ellen was glad that Lawrence Trotter had disregarded her during church services. He detected that there was something betwixt her and Nathan.

Little did she realize that in the interim, her application had been reviewed for consideration of the teaching position at Oldwood College. There had been discussion amongst the school board that decided in favor of offering Mary Ellen the teaching position as they sought to include a few people of color for their feasibility study.

Another deciding factor was taken under consideration. The Livingston Detective Agency was in receipt of Nathan's request for their services. They never turned anyone down if the money was right as they prided themselves on their slogan, '*The Justice Avengers. We take matters into our own hands to see that justice is served!*' They had transmitted an immediate wire to their local agency to contact *Mr. Nathan Jonah Hickey* in person to initiate the process.

Nathan was in the corral watering the horses and singing. Every now and then he would glance at the mansion in hopes of seeing Mary Ellen.

He heard the sound of a horse approaching and turned to see who it was. He didn't recognize the man. He was a Anglo-American man clad in western attire. Nathan approached the gate.

The man addressed him. "Howdy. I'm looking for a Nathan Jonah Hickey."

Nathan's countenance took on a serious expression. "Well you've found him. What can I do for you sir?"

He dismounted, approached the gate, and extended his gloved hand. "I'm Dusty Butler. I'm with the Livingston Detective Agency."

Nathan shook his hand and opened the gate for him to strap his horse.

"Is there some place where we can talk?"

Nathan swallowed hard. "Come with me."

He had waited a long time for this moment. And for some reason, Nathan didn't look pleased that the stranger was there. He told himself that this is what he dreamed about doing for some time now. Nevertheless, why didn't it feel right? This was the day that he awaited to requite the murderers. Somehow, he didn't react the way he had anticipated. Why wasn't he happy to see Dusty Butler?

He escorted Dusty to the carriage house. They sat across from one another. Dusty sat in the chair smiling with his vivid blue eyes and blondish hair. He spoke with a gruff voice, "Son, I know you're glad you've hired us so that you can finally put this behind you. You know we have a solid reputation for...."

Before he had a chance to finish his sentence, Nathan interrupted him as he sat on his davenport with his hands interlocked. He spoke hesitantly, "I wasn't expecting you so soon. I think I need just a little more time to think about this. I mean this is a major step for me." He sighed and lowered his head.

Dusty leaned forward and cleared his throat. He was a large husky man that was badly in need of a shave. "What do you mean? Don't you want to get those cold-blooded sons of—?"

Nathan abruptly interrupted him before he could finish. "I'd appreciate it if you wouldn't use that language here," as his breathing intensified. Nathan developed a piercing look in his eyes and continued. "I need more time to give this some thought. I've looked forward to this moment for months and now that it's here," he nodded sideways, "I'm not sure how I feel at this point." Nathan removed his hat and rubbed his forehead.

Dusty stroked his whiskers and tightened his lips. After releasing his breath of frustration he countered, "So what are you saying? Do you want your folks to lie cold in their graves knowing that they're never gonna get vengeance?"

Nathan's eyes became glassy and before he could respond, he reminded himself of a passage of Scripture that his father used to quote from Jeremiah 51:36: *Therefore thus saith the LORD; Behold, I will plead thy cause, and take vengeance for thee.*

"Sir I'm sorry that you made the trip here—."

Dusty interrupted, "Tell you what son; I'll give you some time to think about it. In the meantime, I'll keep your information handy."

Nathan rose to his feet and proceeded to the door. Dusty understood his non-verbal message. He lifted his barrel-chested body from the chair and grunted, "Up! Well, gotta go."

Nathan escorted him to his horse and watched as he rode away. When Dusty left his viewpoint, he looked toward the mansion to see whether Mary Ellen had noticed.

Nathan mounted Midnight and prepared to take a ride toward the brook until he spotted Mary Ellen. She was dressed in a pastel green calico dress with dark green printed designs. Her hair was parted across the back with a bun atop while the remaining hair draped down her back. She had stepped out on the front verandah. He dismounted and walked over to her. He quickly ascended the two steps and propped himself against the pillar. He couldn't stop himself from grinning for a while.

She grinned at him while their eyes lit up. They chuckled at one another and then Nathan gave her a big hug. "I missed you so much. I know this is wrong, but I looked forward to you ending your consecration. I counted each day."

They laughed again and then it ceased as they peered deeply into one another's eyes. He kissed her lips sweetly. Mama Mae walked to the front door unnoticed and eased away with a look of approval. She prevented the other sisters from disturbing them.

He grabbed her hands and assisted her off the verandah. "Ride with me."

He ran with her hand clasped in his while she clutched the side of her dress with the other and did her best to keep up with him. Finally, nearly out of breath she spoke, "Slow down." He lifted her and carried her inside the corral. She clutched the gate and leaned to catch her breath.

"I didn't know that you could run that fast. I should've known because you're tall." She sucked wind.

He smiled. "My apology. I suppose I run fast because I'm always chasing horses. I've captured wild stallions and sometimes I help Mr. Pope and Mr. John with the cattle. I've roped cattle too."

Mary Ellen looked at him in admiration.

He asked, "Do you want to ride with me or would you prefer to ride Rain?"

"I'll ride Rain because you rode her the other day and I want her to get used to me riding her instead of you."

He nodded in agreement. "It would help if you'd come here and brush her sometimes and feed her—you know form a bond. That is if you wouldn't mind doing something like that."

"I don't mind a bit." He was amazed at her response.

Mary Ellen walked over to Rain and mounted her. She observed Nathan as he whistled for Midnight. Midnight trotted over to him. She was in awe.

"How'd you get him to respond to you like that?"

"It takes patience and training. You have to train your horse to come to you by doing something nice like give it a carrot. And you have to repeat this until the horse gets used to coming to you when you signal for it. And you have to use the same signal like whistle, or something that it'll get used to."

"I think that I can do that."

"You have to be consistent and never ever call a horse to do something that it doesn't like. I'll help you."

She approved. "I'd like that."

Nathan unlatched the gate and pushed it open. He walked Midnight out and waited for Mary Ellen to exit the corral. Nathan looked up and saw Mr. John standing on the side of the mansion. Mr. John beckoned Mary Ellen to come.

Nathan and Mary Ellen returned and sat on the swing on the verandah. Mr. John approached them and patted Nathan's shoulder. "I haven't seen you two together in a while. I thought maybe y'all decided to hem and haw again."

He handed a letter to Mary Ellen and took some parcels inside for Mama Mae. Mary Ellen flipped the envelope over to see where it came from. Her countenance dropped as she nervously opened the letter. Nathan observed her behavior as his eyes squinted.

"Is everything alright?"

She read the contents of the letter and looked at Nathan. Her eyes saddened.

"What is it sweetheart?"

Mary Ellen became uneasy and she handed him the letter. She nervously wrung her fingers. It was a letter of acceptance from Oldwood College. The dean requested her to report to work beginning with the fall term and expects her arrival at the beginning of summer so that she can established herself in Ohio and become acclimated with their school policies and curricula.

After Nathan finished reading the letter, they both lowered their heads.

"I suppose that you'll be leaving us in a month or so. What's it like in Ohio?"

She could barely respond as she fought back the tears. He rubbed her hand and spoke in a gentle tone. "As much as I love you, I wouldn't want to keep you from doing something that's in your heart to do. You enjoy writing and you want to teach others and that's a good thing."

Their eyes were glossy. "What about you? What are you going to do?"

"I don't know. I've been doing some thinking while you were consecrating. I've come to realize that I enjoy my work here at Beauford Place. The people here are kind to me, my wages are decent, and I like what I do. I'm a cowboy—a ranchman and that's what I do best."

She stared at his hand on hers and spoke slowly in a sad monotone manner. "You asked me about Ohio. It's mostly cold during the fall to the spring and sometimes through the majority of the spring season. The ice usually doesn't melt until around late April or early May and then there's usually three months of heat. After that, the cycle repeats itself."

"Doesn't sound like my kind of place. I'd be working outside in brutal weather most of the year. Do you like it there?"

Mary Ellen gazed into his eyes and answered, "No. I like it here. Beauford's always been my home. I hated being away at college, but I would tell myself that it was only temporary."

Nathan stood, looked outward at the land, and placed his hand around his chin. She didn't understand his abruptness as she looked up at him. "Nathan what is it?"

He didn't respond but turned around and walked inside the mansion. Mary Ellen was stunned at his behavior. She stood and paused a moment. She didn't know whether to follow him. Therefore, she chose to wait for him to return to the verandah.

She resumed her seated position on the swing, lowered her head, clasped her hands on the sides of her face, and closed her eyes. After a while, she drifted off to sleep. She was awakened after a while when she heard a tumult that startled her.

Mary Ellen quickly rose to her feet, turned around, and shrieked, "What's going on?"

Nathan stepped out of the mansion to the verandah along with Mr. John, Mama Mae, Jack, Mae, and Marva.

Mary Ellen's eyes enlarged as Nathan beckoned for her to calm down with his hands.

He spoke, "Have a seat." She sat down as well as the others with the exception of himself, Mr. John, and Jack.

Nathan continued, "I have an idea. You want to teach but you don't like Ohio and you don't want to leave

Beauford Place. We can build a schoolhouse on this land and you can teach right here at home."

Mary Ellen's eyes lit up and her lips slightly parted while the others smiled.

Mama Mae added, "You can teach people right here 'cause they sure ain't gettin' a decent education and many of them can't even read or write. Their folks can't afford to send them to good schools and some of the schools don't allow them there even if they could afford it."

Nathan carefully studied Mary Ellen's expression, as he didn't want to upset her.

A serene looked appeared on her as she responded, "I'd love to. I believe daddy would be proud that I'm giving something back to our people and the community—a legacy." Nathan questioned Mary Ellen as he desired for her to be certain. His brows rose. "Are you sure that this is something you'd like to do because you'll be turning down a chance to teach at a college? I just want you to be happy with or without me."

Mr. John patted Nathan's shoulder and Mama Mae spoke up, "She ain't gonna be happy without you."

Mary Ellen uttered, "That's true," that caused Nathan to smile, as he looked starry-eyed.

Mr. John spoke, "So does this mean that we can take care of everything to start the schoolhouse? Because I'll have to drive your mama into town to take care of the paperwork. And Nathan's going to have to go with Mr. Pope to the sawmill."

Mary Ellen looked up at Nathan. "Would you be willing to do all of this for me?"

"Girl, I would ride the meanest, orneriest, toughest bronco for you. I'd sail the seven seas for you."

Everyone burst into laughter with the exception of Nathan. Mary Ellen detected the sincerity in his eyes. She stood and hugged Nathan. Afterwards, she turned around and addressed everyone. "I have a suggestion. Let's name the schoolhouse *Benjamin Beauford* after daddy."

Everyone clapped at her suggestion as they had reached an accord.

Nathan sat on the swing with his arm around Mary Ellen. The others had returned inside. Mary Ellen along with her family was happy concerning her decision. They had desired to do something special to commemorate Benjamin for a long time as no one had thought about naming a schoolhouse after him. It took a cowboy to see her potential to do something fulfilling and rewarding.

"Are you still up to taking a ride?"

She responded, "Yes. But I've kept you from your chores." He smiled. "We don't work around the clock. I usually get up early and—."

She placed her hand over his mouth, "I know you wake up early. Remember I can hear your singing. And speaking of singing, why were you always singing love songs? Have you ever been in love before me?"

He chuckled. "Now what kind of a question is that? The answer is no. I've never been in love before. I did go to a hooch-cooch show once after a trail drive and that's enough of that. Remember, I was raised in the church. My parents didn't let me out of their sight. They were very strict."

He suddenly reminded himself of Dusty's visit and told himself that he hoped that Dusty would never return to Beauford Place or contact him again.

They walked hand-in-hand to their steeds, mounted, and rode toward the direction of the small bridge.

Chapter Eleven

Mary Ellen stood on the bridge and watched the ripples in the water. Nathan gathered more wildflowers and handed them to her. He looked deep into her eyes. She became bewildered.

"I asked you to ride out here with me for a reason."

Her look of bewilderment intensified.

He kneeled and grabbed her hand. "Will you marry me?"

She trembled and placed her hands over her mouth as the wildflowers dropped on him. He brushed them off and stood as he awaited her response.

"Does this mean that you're not going to carry out your mission?"

He sighed. "I can't promise you that. Right now, I'm just trying to be strong and not focus on it."

She stared in his eyes. "You need to resolve this in your heart before we can marry. I love you and I'd love to have you for a husband. You're a kind wonderful man and I know you love me. But your life doesn't exemplify Christ."

"I understand. Sweetheart I'm trying really hard to deal with this. You have no idea as to how hard." He sighed. "A man came to visit me today from the Livingston Detective Agency. I've waited a long time for this moment and somehow it just didn't feel right. I didn't feel right about it. I had a bad feeling."

She placed her hands on his. "What didn't feel right to you?"

"First of all, I didn't care for his attitude. The other reason is that I need more time to think this through. At first, I didn't need any time because my mind was made up. But now things have changed."

She entreated him. "Then why can't you just let it go? Your parents were saved and I know that they didn't believe in being vengeful and they wouldn't want you to be vengeful!" She blotted her eyes with the side of her finger.

He stepped aside, turned around, gripped the sides of the bridge railing, and stared straight ahead. She turned around and placed her hand on his back. His breathing had increased.

"Mary Ellen, I never told you that I was there when it happened. I saw the look on my mother's face. She lunged right in front of my father to prevent him from being killed and they killed him anyway. I saw my mother beg them not to harm him. My father shoved me to safety right before he closed his eyes."

She sniffed as she had no idea of the intensity of his pain and suffering and then asked, "What about us?"

"What do you mean?" His brows rose.

She became frustrated and questioned him firmly. "What's going to happen to us if you decide to carry out your mission? Do you honestly expect me to wait for you forever while you're in prison?" Mary Ellen looked upon him steadfast and assumed a stance with her hands positioned around her hips and feet spread apart as she shifted her weight on her right hip.

He replied with a sheepish tone as he leaned against the bridge, "No. I wouldn't expect you to do something like that."

"How is it that you expect me to marry you? I can't marry you unless you're saved. Otherwise, we'll be unequally yoked. You know all about the order of God. You were raised in the church—remember?"

He turned around and faced her. She looked up at Nathan, scrutinized him, and realized that he's very manly and has the potential to attract many women.

"You told me that you would sail the seven seas for me and I can't even get you to cross over from your past so that we can have a future together as husband and wife!"

His eyes appeared as if he was pleading for help. "Dusty let me know that he would check back with me."

"Who's Dusty? Is that the man that came to visit you?"

He nodded and lowered his eyes. "Yes."

She gave him a stern look. "Nathan we can't further this relationship unless you resolve this issue. In the meantime, I'm going to start preparing lesson plans and become the school mistress for *The Benjamin Beauford Schoolhouse.*"

She walked a few paces and turned around. "Thanks for the suggestion of the schoolhouse. I really appreciate that and I know that daddy would've too. He liked you a lot, you know."

A disgruntled Mary Ellen grasped the sides of her dress as she scurried toward her mare. She quickly mounted Rain and proceeded in the direction of the stables. Nathan bowed himself on the bridge and cried out to God for help as he pounded his fist.

Nathan had awakened bright and early. He was dressed in his cowboy attire and wore chaps over his canvas trousers with spurs on his boots. He helped Mr. Pope to brand cattle as the atmosphere smelled of a mixture of burnt flesh and hair, which was repulsive. Nonetheless, Nathan had grown accustomed to the odor.

Mr. John drove Mama Mae into town to file the necessary paperwork so that Mary Ellen could become the school marm at the schoolhouse. Mary Ellen worked on compiling a list of materials, books, and supplies for the schoolhouse. She also drafted a letter thanking Oldwood College for their offer and graciously turned them down. She told herself that there was just one final touch that was needed—Nathan.

Mary Ellen needed a break from working in the study and decided to sit on the front verandah and get some fresh air. She noticed Nathan sitting near the stables as he whittled a piece of wood. He had gotten himself cleaned up because he anticipated seeing her. He looked up, saw her sitting on the verandah swing, and walked over.

He tipped his hat, "Afternoon."

She responded, "Good afternoon." Mary Ellen hadn't anticipated his visit as she told herself that he was probably busy.

He leaned against the pillar and continued to whittle. She patted the seat of the chair. "Have a seat."

He smiled at her and sat down. "How's your day going?"

She returned the smile. "Everything's going fine so far. I started my list for everything that I need for the schoolhouse—or at least everything that I can think of for now. I'm certain that my list will expand. What about you?"

"I branded cattle all morning with Mr. Pope."

"What you got there?"

He looked down. "It's just a little something that I made for you."

He handed her a small wooden cross that he had whittled. It had a hole to string a chain through. Mary Ellen untied a satin ribbon from her braid and loosened her hair. She strung the ribbon through the hole and held the cross up by the two ends of the ribbon to show him.

He smiled. "That looks nice."

"I need for you to tie it around my neck." She handed it to him, pulled her hair up, and turned around. He tied it around her neck. She lowered her hair, repositioned herself on the swing, and admired her cross. "Thank you."

She knew that Nathan felt bad. "Would you like to have lunch with me? I could have Miss Edna to pack us something and I can spread a blanket on the side of the house and we can eat—or we can eat out here on the verandah."

"I'd love to have lunch with you. Here or on the side of the house is fine with me."

Mary Ellen stood and placed her hand on his shoulder while she opened the door. "I'll be right back."

Nathan helped her spread a blanket on the ground. She placed the basket on the blanket and handed him a plate along with eating utensils. They ate southern fried chicken, rolls, and fresh fruit. They chuckled as they took bites from their chicken.

Nathan spoke, "I know your family irritates you by the way they act at the supper table. But I must admit, Miss Beatrice does wonders with her cooking. I haven't had fried chicken like this in a long time."

She laughed and looked at him in admiration. She told herself that she's trusting God to soften his heart. She told herself that he would make a good husband.

"So when do you plan to visit the sawmill?"

"Mr. John mentioned something about possibly going tomorrow because he had to take your mother into town to get some paperwork filed for you to be able to teach here. If he can't go, I'll take Mr. Pope along."

She swallowed her food and then responded, "You know, I'm really looking forward to having my own schoolhouse!" She clenched her fists and shook them, as she was elated. "I praise God that things are finally coming together." She sighed and curled her bottom lip while staring at him.

Nathan knew the reason that she had given him that look. She desired a true commitment from him as did the Lord.

He swallowed the bite of chicken that he had relished on as if it was a juicy rib eye.

"I've been up most of the night contemplating on what you said to me yesterday at the bridge. I need to take care of something and I'm asking you to be patient with me just for a few more days—please."

She looked at him with doleful eyes that he found irresistible. "I expect you to keep your promise and don't renege."

He knew in his heart that he didn't want to lose her. Therefore he spoke, "I promise."

After they finished enjoying their lunch, she tossed some breadcrumbs to the birds and squirrels. He looked at her in admiration. "You're a beautiful lady. You have such a caring spirit and that's what I love about you the most. I never would've believed in a million years that you would've returned my love. That's a miracle to me."

Mama Mae stomped up the two steps affixed to the front verandah and Mr. John followed.

"Mama what's the matter?" Mary Ellen followed her inside. She tossed her purse on the parlor davenport and sat down. Miss Edna entered the room. "Baby get me some water please." Miss Edna scurried to the kitchen.

Mary Ellen looked at Mr. John. "What's wrong with mama?"

He snorted and jerked his arm. "They told her that they want you to write a speech and a poem so that they can decide whether they'll approve you to teach!"

Mama Mae interrupted and spoke sorrowful. "And they want it the day after tomorrow! They didn't give you no time to prepare! They claim they want to finalize everything concerning school this week."

Mary Ellen turned and looked at Nathan who had stepped inside from the verandah. "Did you hear that?"

Nathan gently placed his hands on her shoulders. "You can do it baby. You've got it in you." She smiled.

Mr. John interrupted, "And that's not all. They said they want you to come to town and give your speech and recite your poem right in front of them!"

Mary Ellen looked at her mother. "Mama, I'll do it. I did it before at Oldwood. I'll get started on it right away and we'll ride back into town. I'll write something and present it to them."

She walked over to Mama Mae, kissed her on the cheek, and hugged her. Mary Ellen turned and repositioned herself to face everyone as her sisters had entered the room along with Jack.

"After I prepare my speech and write my poem, I'd like for all of you to listen and give me your opinion before I present it to them."

Everyone verbally agreed.

Nathan developed a look in his eyes as if he had been brainstorming. His eyes squinted, "What about the poem that you wrote at your Alma Mater? You know the one that you told me about that the college published."

Mary Ellen's eyes widened and her lips slightly parted. Nathan had done it again! "Why didn't I think of that? Now all I need to do is focus on my speech."

Mary Ellen and Nathan stood on the verandah that evening. He placed his arms around her while they appreciated the sunset in its grandeur and one another. Nathan reassured her. "Don't worry about a thing, sweetness." She leaned her head against his chest.

That evening, she stepped out on the verandah outside of her bedroom as she watched her beau walk to the carriage house. Her heart was fixed that she would trust the Lord to work everything out and get them over the hurdles that they faced. She drew a deep breath and took time to appreciate God and all His blessings bestowed upon her. Afterwards, she pivoted, returned inside, and prepared herself for bed.

Mary Ellen sat at the large desk in the study bright and early in the morning. She had drafted a few pages of her speech, reviewed it, and penned numerous revisions. She rewrote it a second time today as she sat in the large leather chair on wheels. She stopped writing for a few minutes and leaned back in the chair. She looked toward a corner of the desk and admired a framed black and white photograph of her parents when they were younger. Afterwards, she focused her attention on a framed painted portrait of her mother that hung on the wall. Mama Mae was young and beautiful. She could see traits of herself in the portrait.

She noticed something in the corner that she hadn't paid attention to. Her father's black cowboy hat hung on a hat rack in one corner of the study. She had completely forgotten that her father used to wear a cowboy hat when he was younger. She reminded herself that this was the reason that Nathan reminded her so much of her father. Her father didn't think that it was beneath him to be a ranchman. Her mother told her that Benjamin was fond of Nathan and that's why he hired him.

She observed another smaller black and white photograph positioned on a mahogany table next to a burgundy leather armchair. It was her father dressed in a black cowboy outfit wearing his cowboy hat standing beside a beautiful steed. She emerged from the chair, walked to the table, and examined the picture. He was handsome like Nathan when he was younger. A closed-mouth smile stretched across her face. She returned the photograph to its original position and resumed her seated position behind the desk.

Mary Ellen skillfully scanned the contents of her speech and made some additional edits. After carefully reviewing the contents for accuracy a third time, she was ready to begin typing. She eyed the black high-back steel typewriter with its stair-step style rounded keys. She repositioned it in front of her, inserted a sheet of paper, and typed. Mary Ellen was self-taught to type, as she loved to scribe and type her final work.

She knew in her heart that she preferred to see Nathan today. However, she had to remain focused as she continued to prepare, pray, and rehearse her presentation.

Chapter Twelve

Mary Ellen told herself that today was the day! She decided not to join the family for an early morning breakfast, which was not the usual and customary timeframe for the Beauford household with the exception of Sunday mornings. They had to be up and about early today and prepare to ride into town.

She had rehearsed her speech aforetime until she couldn't bear to read it anymore. Mary Ellen detested the ride into town and was overjoyed that she had reached her destination—that was until a knot formed in her stomach. She questioned herself, what if she doesn't receive her approval? Mary Ellen retrieved her small Bible from her purse and read some Scriptures for reassurance. She had missed seeing Nathan prior to her departure into town.

Mr. John assisted her from the carriage and then helped Mama Mae. Mary Ellen did her best to ignore the townspeople that gazed upon them in awe, as they were wealthy. She rubbed her well-tailored Victorian style walking skirt suit with her hands to readjust it prior to entering the building. She chose to wear a royal blue two-piece walking skirt suit with a fitted full button jacket and matching rear-bustled overskirt, which fit her perfectly. Atop her head sat a ladies' straw boater with hanging fabric to protect the back of her neck from the sun. Her hair was pinned underneath in a bouffant coiffure.

Mama Mae had slept throughout their journey. She was exhausted from making the journey into town the day before yesterday, as she was unaccustomed to waking up early on a weekday. Mama Mae rubbed her eyes, drew a deep breath, and looked at her daughter in admiration. "Well baby this is it. Make us proud. And don't you worry 'cause I've been praying and God's in control."

Mary Ellen smiled as she reached up and fixed Mama Mae's hair. "Oh child I probably look a sight." She immediately reached into her purse, retrieved a compact, and pushed the sides of her hair as she viewed her appearance.

Mr. John cleared his throat as he had returned from parking the carriage. "Ladies it's time for us to go inside and see what these people have to say."

They entered the building and were greeted by the same man from their previous visit. Mr. John spoke up. "Good morning Mr. Friedlander."

He was a stout moustached man that wore rounded wire-rimmed spectacles. Mr. Friedlander didn't smile. This caused Mary Ellen to feel a bit uneasy. Instead, he spoke firmly as if a script guided him. "Right this way." He extended his arm directing them to an entrance.

Mary Ellen gaped and her eyes enlarged. She looked up and there were numerous Anglo-American men and women seated with grim expressions. The assembly consisted of at least two hundred people. Mr. John and Mama Mae were directed to sit behind them.

Mary Ellen did her best to appear calm as she was escorted on the stage and seated behind the podium. Seated beside her were additional spectators. An older woman stood at the podium. She announced, "Ladies and gentlemen, Mary Ellen Beauford is here to give her presentation."

Mary Ellen swallowed hard as she rose from her seat to approach the podium. She glanced toward the rear at Mama Mae and Mr. John. She reminded herself that she would trust the Lord. She nervously placed her paper on the podium and drew a deep breath. She re-introduced herself by her proper title as *Dr. Mary Ellen Beauford* and smiled albeit no one returned her smile as their faces appeared solemn.

Mary Ellen reiterated her educational credentials and accolades that she had accomplished at Oldwood College because she was uncertain as to what information Mama Mae had provided.

She looked stunning and opulent. She presented her speech grandiloquently. She spoke, "Higher learning is accomplished through education. Without education, one cannot attain the level of expertise in his or her field and broaden their horizons. While education may be vast and challenging, it is very important to obtain for future success. Without education, an individual may be cheated from the opportunities of life.

Education is not limited by age, gender, or creed. An individual can attain education as long as they desire to do so. Education allows an individual to specify and modify career goals whether it is accomplished on a baccalaureate or an advanced degree level. The process of obtaining higher education is one that an individual must have the willpower to endure.

Many have had to postpone their desired level of education due to rearing a family, lack of funds, being denied admission, along with other hardships only to find themselves with a thirst to further their education later in life. There are times when this may be their only recourse. Whereas, others are able to secure their education at a tender age wherein obstacles have been prohibited or are non-existent.

My reason for requesting permission to teach at a schoolhouse is two-fold. Firstly, my father, the late Benjamin Beauford, known by all of you for his farming invention, desired for me to become successful by obtaining higher education. Secondly, my desire is to teach others that cannot attend school in town. Therefore, I desire to have a schoolhouse erected at Beauford Place, dedicate it to my father, and teach others.

I was afforded an opportunity to teach at Oldwood College in Ohio. While I found their offer to be gracious, my family, and I would like to positively affect others in this state as we were blessed to have the means to do so.

Therefore, if I am granted this approval, I pledge to adhere to your policies and provide current books and supplies for the schoolhouse."

Mary Ellen glanced at her mother and continued. "I have chosen to recite a poem that I had written that was published by my Alma Mater. It is titled *Education*." She recited her poem from memory and made eye contact with everyone that she could.

"Education is life's pathway to learning,
While faith is the key to answer my yearning.
Hope is my beacon that shines a bright light,
Prayer is the answer as I long to do right.

Expansion of knowledge is something to treasure,
While studying mathematics and learning to measure.
The field of science provokes one to wonder,
How lightning strikes and what causes thunder.

Education produces lawyers and doctors,
As well as valuable educational proctors.
Science explains refracted light through a prism,
Instead of suffering bondage brought about by schism.

Literature, science, mathematics, and chemistry,
Can cause one to create and develop an industry.
Therefore learning should not be a mystery,
It should become a part of one's history.

Because learning has no gender, color or creed,
It's willing to avail itself to all in need.
Therefore open wide the gates of education,
And fill the house on the day of graduation."

After Mary Ellen concluded her eloquent delivery, her heart raced as she observed the reactions of those that studied her. She was ready to get out of there. Mama Mae clapped and cheered while the others appeared stiff as they sat erect with the exception of Mr. John who appeared discouraged. He leaned over and whispered to Mama Mae, "What's wrong with these people? They didn't even clap."

Mama Mae didn't respond as she slightly rocked sideways and hummed a hymnal to sooth her spirit. Mary Ellen was escorted out of the assembly where she met Mama Mae and Mr. John as they had waited outside for her to rejoin them. Mama Mae hugged and kissed her.

"Baby I don't know what's wrong with these people. But don't you worry about a thing. No matter what the outcome is I'm proud of you!"

Mr. John hugged her and turned around in time to see Mr. Friedlander. He questioned him. "When will she know their decision?"

He stroked his moustache and responded. "Wait here." Mr. John gave an eye roll and blew his breath in frustration as Mary Ellen and Mama Mae appeared concerned.

Mary Ellen explained, "I was nervous at first."

Mr. John and Mama Mae looked at one another. Mama Mae responded, "We couldn't tell," and Mr. John replied, "No we couldn't," while nodding sideways with his lower lip curled.

Mary Ellen glanced at the entrance leading to the assembly. "I wish he'd hurry up and let us know something so that we can get out of here."

Mr. John escorted Mama Mae to one of the chairs positioned in the lobby. He sat beside Mama Mae and crossed his right leg sideways over his left knee. He placed his hat atop his lap and thumped the wooden armrest.

Mary Ellen remained in her stance. Within a few minutes, Mr. Friedlander returned bustling through the door.

"They're deliberating now. You can wait if you wish or we can mail you our decision or you can return tomorrow."

Mr. John rose from his seated position and approached him. "If we choose to wait, how long do you think they'll be?"

He glanced at his wristwatch and twisted his nose. "Well seeing that it's getting close to lunch time, I'd say that it shouldn't take much longer."

Mr. John turned toward Mama Mae. "Are you feeling up to waiting?"

"I'll stay 'cause I want Little Stockings to have an answer before we leave." She looked tired and fanned herself.

Mr. Friedlander clapped his hands together, pursed his lips, pivoted, and returned inside the assembly. Mary Ellen seated herself comfortably in the chair opposite her mother.

While they awaited an answer, trouble was brewing elsewhere. "What do you mean you won't sell us any lumber?" Mr. Pope's anger intensified as he glared at the sawmill worker. Nathan became bewildered and gently lifted his hand to calm Mr. Pope.

Nathan studied the man and questioned him to ascertain clarification. "Are you saying that you're refusing to sell us lumber?"

The young male Anglo-American employee responded. "This here man said that ya'll was building a schoolhouse. Who gave you permission to build a schoolhouse around these parts?"

Mr. Pope beckoned to Nathan that he was alright and spoke up. "First of all, what we're doing is legal. Secondly, we shouldn't have to explain that to you."

The tall lean employee was uniformed in dungarees with an embroidered patch that read '*Hank.*'

Nathan eyed his patch. "Hank, where's your foreman?"

Hank stammered with his response. "He—he ain't here."

Nathan queried further. "Were you given orders not to sell wood to anyone erecting a schoolhouse?"

Mr. Pope looked at Nathan. Nathan told him, "You shouldn't have mentioned the fact that we were thinking of erecting a schoolhouse. You should've told him that we were erecting a woodshed or something!"

Mr. Pope responded while Hank stared at Nathan. "That would be telling a lie son and a lie is a sin."

Nathan didn't respond as he focused his attention toward Hank who appeared to be nervous. Hank removed his cap, swept his blond hair back, and wiped sweat from his forehead. The sound of a door opening captured their attention. An older man approached them.

"Hank what's the problem out here?"

Hank responded nervously, "Nothing sir. These here fellas want to buy lumber to erect a schoolhouse and I told them that we can't sell it to them."

The older gentleman stood in front of Nathan and Mr. Pope and studied them. Afterwards, he turned toward Hank.

"Where'd you get the notion that we can't sell them any lumber?"

Sweat beads covered Hank's forehead as he mopped his face nervously with his hand. "I—I thought that you wouldn't want to sell them any."

The older gentleman addressed Nathan. Nathan's fixation remained steadfast on him.

"The name's Honeycutt and this here's my sawmill."

Nathan nodded, "Nathan Hickey." He extended his arm toward Mr. Pope. "And this is Mr. Pope and we're here to purchase some lumber."

Mr. Pope added, "Mr. Honeycutt, we're not here to cause any trouble. We just want to purchase some lumber."

Mr. Honeycutt looked at Hank. "Well don't just stand there boy. Fetch these men some lumber!" Nathan followed Hank to give him instructions as to the amount and other supplies that they needed.

"You have to excuse Hank. He has a tendency to become overzealous concerning his duties. I earn my living selling lumber and I can't afford to pick and choose who to sell it to. My old man wasn't that way and neither am I."

This placed Mr. Pope at ease. "That's good to know."

"I've got a pretty good deal on some paint. What color do you plan to paint the schoolhouse?"

Mr. Friedlander burst through the entrance carrying some papers. He startled Mary Ellen who had drifted off to sleep. Mr. John stood. "Well what's the verdict?"

Mr. Friedlander peered at Mary Ellen intensely. Her heart sank. She looked at Mama Mae and Mr. John as she anticipated bad news.

"Well young lady. I've been advised that you've been granted provisionary approval."

Mr. John interrupted him. "What's provisionary?"

Mary Ellen interjected, "Allow him to continue. I understand what provisionary means."

Mr. Friedlander cleared his throat. "As I previously stated, you've been granted provisionary approval. The provision being that you must have the schoolhouse erected no later than the end of May so that we can have an account of available schools for students to attend to notify parents before the close of this school year."

Mary Ellen questioned, "How do you all prefer to receive notification after the schoolhouse is constructed?"

He responded, "You can write me when it's ready and I'll ride out and take a look at it. And if all is well you'll receive your permanent approval papers."

He handed her the papers granting her provisionary approval and shook her hand. "Congratulations. I know you'll do just fine." To everyone's amazement, he managed to muster up a smile at Mary Ellen.

When they exited the building, Mr. John placed his hat on his head and questioned, "Now why couldn't they have done that in the first place instead of putting Little Stockings through all that trouble?"

Mama Mae responded, "You know the reason why and the good Lord knows too."

Mr. John assisted Mary Ellen inside the carriage. She spoke, "Whatever their reasoning is, I thank God for granting provisionary approval. And I don't mind teaching the people in our area because they need to be taught. And I'll see to it that they receive a quality education."

Chapter Thirteen

Mary Ellen anticipated seeing Nathan as it had been a busy day for both of them. She observed the stacks of lumber on the far side of the mansion facing the dirt road. She stepped down from the front verandah, grabbed the sides of her walking skirt, and hastened toward Mr. Pope who was standing near the lumber.

She smiled gingerly. "You've been busy. Did mama tell you that I was granted provisionary approval?"

"She sure did." He smiled and gave her a hug. "You looking for your sweetheart?"

She chuckled. "How'd you know?"

He rolled his eyes and laughed. "He went to get cleaned up."

She chuckled again. "I need to get out of my walking suit and prepare for supper."

Mr. Pope grinned. "Say, what color did you want the schoolhouse? Nate said to get red. So I did."

She smiled. "Red is fine. I like red. What about the inside?"

"We got blue."

"Blue is fine. Well I better get inside and freshen up before Nathan gets here."

They chuckled.

Mary Ellen was grateful to the Lord as she placed a lovely dress across her bed and prepared to bathe. She could smell the aroma of Miss Beatrice's cooking. She hoped that Nathan would join them for supper.

Nathan stood on the front verandah, as his eyes were fixated on Mary Ellen as she exited the front door. She looked lovely in her flowing blue dress. He was dressed in a full dark suit with a matching jacket that came near his knees. He wore a nice western necktie and looked handsome as she recognized her favorite scent of his aftershave. He in turn appreciated her perfumed fragrance. They grimaced at one another with closed mouths. He stood and looked starry-eyed in his appearance.

He extended his hands outward to hold hers and caressed them. And then he lifted her hands and gently kissed them. "I missed you baby."

She smiled. "I missed you too."

He drew her toward him and pleasantly kissed her. And then they abruptly ceased from kissing.

"I think I got a little too carried away." He explained.

"I think so too."

She took his hand and led him to sit on the wooden swing.

"I was blessed to receive provisionary approval to teach at the schoolhouse."

His eyes lit up. "I kinda figured that you had some good news to share. I saw the look in your eyes."

She smiled. "As if your eyes aren't lit up."

He chuckled. "I love you Mary Ellen."

"I love you too." They prepared to kiss again and they quickly drew back as they changed their minds. Instead they looked at one another and laughed.

She patted his knee. "We better get inside so that we can eat."

He stood and assisted her from the swing. They proceeded inside arm-in-arm.

Mary Ellen prepared herself mentally for the family conversational drama at the supper table. Nathan seated her at the table next to him. Mr. John was seated across from Mary Ellen and sat next to Mama Mae. Beside her sat Marva. Mae and Jack sat on the opposite side of Nathan.

Miss Beatrice and Miss Edna entered with savory dishes that consisted of fried pork chops, mashed potatoes, gravy, dressing, and sugar snap peas. Mary Ellen placed a large pork chop on her plate as she had hungered from traveling. Everyone took notice, as she's known to eat very little. Before anyone could say anything she blurted, "I know. I know. I'm really hungry today."

Nathan chuckled and Mama Mae spoke up. "She ain't the only one. We didn't stop anyplace to eat."

Mr. John added, "Ain't that the truth?"

"Well, whose turn is it to bless the food?" Mama Mae eyed everyone at the table.

Jack spoke up, "I'll give it a whirl."

Everyone laughed.

Mama Mae questioned, "And just how do you give prayer a whirl?"

Mae sided with her mother, as she looked puzzled. "I was wondering the same thing."

Mary Ellen interjected, "Well—somebody do something because I'm really hungry today."

Everyone laughed again.

Jack resumed his composure. "Let us bow our heads."

After he finished blessing the food, everyone spoke, "Amen," in unison.

Mary Ellen quickly cut into her pork chop. Nathan looked at her and spoke in a low tone. "Slow down. That pork chop isn't going to get up and walk off your plate."

She smiled and responded, "I was really nervous today. I think it's just nerves."

He patted her hand. "But you got through it like a champion."

"The schoolhouse has to be constructed really fast so that I can receive full approval."

Mae just couldn't help herself as she interrupted them. "Mama told me and Big Stockings about your provisionary approval. She said you did really good when you gave your speech."

Nathan smiled as Mama Mae nodded and interjected, "Yep and she was real professional and all."

Mr. John looked at Nathan and spoke. "We're gonna have to get that schoolhouse erected soon. I say we start on it tomorrow."

Nathan nodded in agreement, as he chewed his food.

Mary Ellen looked up at Mr. John. "Where are we going to get the desks and chairs from?"

Nathan had swallowed his food and answered. "Mr. Pope is taking care of that. The man that we met at the sawmill told him where he could order the desks and chairs."

Mary Ellen added, "I'm placing the order for the textbooks, and a chalkboard, and school supplies."

Marva stopped eating and blotted her mouth. "I think it's a blessing that you decided to stay here and teach because this area could use a good teacher."

Mae interrupted, "I know. I get tired of seeing these young folk around here that can barely read and write."

Mama Mae looked up from her plate and muttered, "It's too bad Ben's not here to see this."

Marva rubbed her mother's back. "Don't worry mama. You know that daddy would be proud of Little Stockings investing something good in this town."

Miss Beatrice arrived with two rhubarb pies as Miss Edna followed with coffee. Mary Ellen was too full to eat another thing. Nathan helped himself to pie and coffee.

The men had spent several days erecting the schoolhouse. Mary Ellen received the supplies and chose to store them in the study until the start of school in the fall. Mr. Pope had the desks and chairs neatly arranged inside the schoolhouse. They had done a magnificent job, as Mama Mae spared no expense. The men had constructed windows on all sides that served a duo purpose. Mary Ellen could have a nice view and she could watch the weather conditions. The schoolhouse could seat fifty pupils. Mary Ellen had sent a letter to Mr. Friedlander to inspect the schoolhouse.

Mary Ellen carried a pitcher of lemonade inside the schoolhouse to the men along with some glasses and placed them on a tray on her desk. She admired her solid oak desk as she rubbed her hand across it. She looked around the classroom and appreciated the craftsmanship. Nathan stepped inside and she poured him a glass of lemonade. He was dressed in denim overalls.

"Thanks."

After he took a swallow, he admired the classroom and looked at Mary Ellen. "So what do you think?"

Mary Ellen smiled. "I think it's beautiful." She looked like a school marm dressed in a floor-length navy blue skirt along with a high-collared buttoned blouse with leg-o-mutton sleeves. Around her neck hung the cross that Nathan had whittled for her.

The classroom had a coatroom, built-in shelving for books, and a wood-burning stove to heat the classroom during cool days. The schoolhouse featured a bell atop and a foyer at the front entrance.

The family gathered outside along with Bishop E.G. Bronnum and watched as Nathan stood on a ladder and affixed a sign that read *Benjamin Beauford Schoolhouse.* He also affixed a sign indicating the year that the schoolhouse was erected. After Nathan climbed down Bishop spoke, "Let us all gather together in prayer so that we can dedicate this building to the Lord and ask His blessing to be upon it."

Miss Beatrice, Miss Edna, Mr. Pope, and Mr. John gathered along with Nathan and the family. Nathan clasped Mary Ellen's hand as they bowed their heads.

The Bishop prayed, *"Heavenly Father in the mighty name of Jesus, we thank thee O' Lord for blessing us with this school. We also thank You for the courage of Sister Mary Ellen Beauford to accept Your will in her life and to give of herself unselfishly to teach the disadvantaged youth. I ask that You bless the work of her hands and give her wisdom and guidance as we dedicate and commit this building into Your hands. I ask that You would bless this family that is represented here this day O' Lord including the faithful workers on this property. Lord further this school and bless each and every student that attends here. In Jesus' name I pray. Let everyone say,"* They responded in unison, *"Amen."*

Bishop Bronnum hugged Mama Mae as tears welled in her eyes. He shook Mary Ellen's hand. "Congratulations. I know you'll do fine."

She smiled. "Thank you."

Bishop Bronnum noticed Nathan standing close to her and shook his hand. He glanced at Mary Ellen, returned his focus toward Nathan, and smiled at them. "I'm Bishop Bronnum."

Nathan peered into his eyes. "Nathan Hickey. It's nice to meet you sir."

"It's nice to meet you. I've never seen you at church. Stop by and visit us sometime."

Mama Mae escorted Bishop Bronnum inside to view the classroom. Everyone followed them and was surprised to see that Nathan had hung a nice picture of Benjamin Beauford on the back wall—all except Mama Mae who had given Nathan a nice framed painting of her late husband. Mama Mae placed her hand on Nathan's shoulder and spoke, "You did good son."

Mr. John peered out of one of the classroom windows and noticed that Mr. Friedlander had finally arrived. "That Friedlander fella is here."

Mary Ellen smiled and blurted in excitement, "Thank God," and rushed out to greet him. She had scheduled his inspection for that day with hopes that he would arrive before or after the blessing of the schoolhouse.

Mr. Friedlander climbed out of his buggy, placed his hand above his brows to block the sunlight, and looked onward at the schoolhouse in amazement.

"Hello Mr. Friedlander. I'm glad that you were able to get here today."

He looked at Mary Ellen and shook her hand. "I'm surprised that you were able to have it erected within the timeframe. I wish that everyone was as dedicated as you are."

He was dressed in a dark suit. He reached inside his suit jacket and retrieved his wire-rimmed rounded spectacles as they proceeded to the schoolhouse. Mary Ellen noticed that there was something different about him and dared to query. "You look somewhat different from when we first met."

He chuckled as he rubbed underneath his nose. "I shaved my moustache."

Mary Ellen's brows tightened. "So that's what it is. I knew that something was different."

"I thought if I shaved it off that I'd look more distinguished."

Mary Ellen smiled at him. "Well you do."

He returned the smile. "Thank you."

He looked up at the sign on the schoolhouse and stepped inside. He marveled as he studied the craftsmanship and the furnishings. He approached Mama Mae, shook her hand, and then shook Mr. John's hand as he remembered his visitation to the building.

"You all did a superb job here."

Mary Ellen's eyes lit up. "Does this mean that I can receive my full approval?"

"Yes it does. I have your authorization papers here and I also brought along the approval that your mother applied for to operate as an independent school."

Mama Mae raised her hands and rejoiced while Mary Ellen shook Mr. Friedlander's hand. Mary Ellen noticed that Nathan was standing in the doorway and hugged him excitedly as he lifted her up. Afterwards, she shook Mr. Friedlander's hand again. "Thank you sir."

Mama Mae blurted, "Can I offer you something to eat or drink?"

He shook Mama Mae's hand. "I'll gladly take something to drink and I'll be on my way so that I can make it back in time for supper."

Mama Mae spoke, "Come with me."

Everyone had left the schoolhouse with the exception of Mary Ellen and Nathan. Mary Ellen peered into his eyes, as she still desired for him to make a decision to totally commit to God and their relationship.

He looked intensely at her as if he knew what she was going to ask. He leaned against the front entrance and was dressed in cowboy attire.

"Are you going to accept Bishop Bronnum's invitation to church?"

He appeared as if he didn't have the words to respond. "I've asked that you be patient with me because I'm still trying to sort some things out."

She walked over and leaned against the wall beside him. "Nathan I need some type of commitment from you. I don't want you to be just my suitor. And you know that I can't marry you if you're unsaved. In fact, I won't marry you or anyone else that's unsaved!"

He looked downward as his cowboy hat covered his eyes. "I realize that and I'm still struggling with something right now. I just need more time."

She placed her hand under his chin and gently lifted his head. "I love you very much. But I won't keep waiting."

Chapter Fourteen

Mary Ellen chose not to dine with Nathan or her family that evening. Nathan decided against joining the family for supper as he didn't want to face Mary Ellen. She had eaten a small portion of food earlier in the kitchen with Miss Beatrice. Mary Ellen realized that she had to put her foot down or end their relationship although they loved one another. She stepped out on her verandah outside of her bedroom. She wore a long robe, had it tied around her, and began to talk to God as she clutched the railing and lowered her head.

"Lord You've brought us this far. And You know that I can't marry Nathan without him receiving You. And You know that he's still struggling with thoughts of carrying out his mission to avenge his parents. I don't know what else to do at this point except trust You as best I can. My faith has wavered and I need Your help."

She paused briefly as her eyes watered. "Lord thank You for opening doors to allow me to teach here. I love You Jesus. You are so magnificent. Thank You for bringing me through my speech before the board and committee members."

She sighed and looked toward the carriage house. "Lord I love him and I need for You to touch his heart."

Mary Ellen stared up at the stars and drew a deep breath. She missed having supper with Nathan and told herself that she would back off for a bit.

Nathan prepared himself for bed as he climbed in wearing his long johns and draped the covers around him. He reached for Mary Ellen's picture that was positioned on his night stand. He stared at her picture every evening before he would allow himself to fall asleep. He kissed her picture and spoke softly, "Good night sweetness."

Afterwards, he repositioned it on his nightstand, put his light out, clutched his pillow, and drifted off to sleep.

It was a sunny Saturday morning and Mary Ellen had awakened bright and early as she had grown accustomed to doing so. She noticed that there was something missing—Nathan's crooning. She asked herself why he wasn't singing as he had done habitually in times past.

Nonetheless, she was elated at the fact that Mama Mae received the approval to operate the schoolhouse independently and that she received approval to teach. She was especially happy that the schoolhouse had been erected. What a wonderful way to begin her weekend.

After Mary Ellen refreshed herself and dressed, she descended down the stairs. She knew in her heart that she missed Nathan and tried to be strong. She walked through the downstairs to see whether anyone had awakened. She knew that Mama Mae would sleep in as she was tired and weary from the events from yesterday.

Mary Ellen desired to sit on the front verandah. Nevertheless, she didn't want to face Nathan although she missed hearing his soothing voice and seeing his eyes sparkle. She told herself that perhaps he wasn't around as there was no sign of him. She clutched the sides of her floor-length yellow dress and stepped out on the verandah. Her long black crinkly hair hung loosely draped around her shoulders and down her back. She positioned herself comfortably on the swing and crossed her legs while she rocked the swing with her foot. She shut her eyes and was glad to enjoy a relaxing morning after the stressful events that she had recently experienced. She had watched the men erect the schoolhouse in addition to when she had given her speech and awaited approval. It was finally over.

It was a little too quiet around there. Nathan had made an indelible impression upon her. She could barely remain in her relaxed state because she wondered where Nathan was. Mary Ellen finally stood and looked over at the stables. She longed to take a ride on Rain with Nathan riding Midnight alongside of her but told herself that she could do without a horse ride today.

She told herself that he probably slept in which was unusual. There was no sign of Miss Beatrice. Therefore, she couldn't question her as to whether Nathan had her to prepare breakfast for him. Miss Beatrice usually prepared breakfast for the staff in her quarters and would walk across to the mansion to cook around the time when the family would awaken.

Mary Ellen decided to walk across the property to the schoolhouse and look around since she didn't have a chance to admire it without interruption. As she approached the schoolhouse, she looked onward and appreciated the sign that Nathan had affixed to it. She also noticed something that she hadn't paid attention to and then realized that there were additional embellishments. There were rectangular shaped planters affixed beneath the window ledges that contained freshly planted flowers thus giving the outside of the schoolhouse a nice cottage look. As she approached the doorway, she heard a familiar sound and smiled. She stepped inside the schoolhouse and was stunned to see Nathan busily working inside and crooning.

She couldn't stop herself from smiling and nodded her head sideways. He was clad in denim jeans, a western style blue shirt, a matching neckerchief, a brown cowboy hat, and brown leather boots. The scent of his cologne filled the classroom.

Nathan lifted his hat. "Morning." He continued to work beautifying the schoolhouse.

She replied, "Good morning." It became obvious to Mary Ellen that he didn't appear enthusiastic to see her as his demeanor lacked the zeal that he normally displayed.

Rejection wasn't her strong suit. Therefore, Mary Ellen tried to make polite conversation, as she desired him to show her special attention. "What are you doing working in here so early?"

He didn't smile nor make eye contact and continued to work. "I just thought that you would enjoy having fresh flowers to look at."

She wasted a smile. "Thank you. I noticed the lovely flowers."

Mary Ellen maintained her stance with her head lowered and arms folded as she watched him tack molding around the edges where the wooden floor and wall met while on his knees. She became embittered by the banging sound of his hammer. She didn't want him to feel begrudged from their conversation of the previous day. An impasse certainly existed between them and she had become irritated by his nonchalance.

She finally decided to give up as she understood the unpleasantness of experiencing rejection now that the shoe was on the other foot so-to-speak. "I guess I'll leave you to your work."

Mary Ellen turned around to depart and she noticed that the hammering had ceased. She heard him when he approached her.

"Let me show you something." He took her hand and escorted her outside to the building to show her the newly constructed privy adjacent to the schoolhouse. It was a contemporary styled privy similar to a water closet, which was another one of Mama Mae's generous contributions.

A smile emerged on her face and not due to the construction of the privy. "It's nice."

He looked at her. "I didn't get a chance to show it to you yesterday because you left."

Embarrassment swept over her face as Mary Ellen knew that she had left abruptly yesterday and refused to have supper with him. His striking eyes always caused her to feel empathetic. She told herself that she would resist them to no avail.

They walked back to the schoolhouse, which was but a stone's throw in distance. He continued to work and she walked over to her father's portrait and admired it. Nathan stopped tacking the molding and worked on tacking a beautifully carved wooden cross on the wall where her desk was positioned. Nathan and Mr. Pope had transported her large blackboard from the study and positioned it in the front of the classroom yesterday.

Mary Ellen turned around as she noticed that the hammering sound wasn't resonating from the direction of the floor. She observed the cross and her eyes watered as she covered her mouth with her hand. He stood back and studied it to assure proper placement. He didn't have to reposition it. Nathan then resumed tacking the molding around the room.

Mary Ellen chose to return to the front verandah so that he could finish as she was satisfied that he still showed concern for her. It was still early for the remainder of her family to awaken. She appreciated knowing that they wouldn't disturb her as she rocked the swing by pressing her right foot against the floor of the verandah.

She repositioned her body to lie across the swing and became comfortable as she drifted off to sleep. About the span of an hour had passed. The sound of a horse's hooves galloping awakened her as she thought it to be Nathan. Mary Ellen slowly eased herself up to prevent falling to the floor. She stood to see who it was. She placed her hand across her brows to block the sun so that she could identify the traveler.

Mary Ellen stepped down and proceeded to the wrought-iron gate. She opened it. It was Dusty Butler from the Livingston Detective Agency. He lifted his cowboy hat.

"Morning ma'am. The name's Dusty Butler and I'm here to see Nathan Hickey. We have business together and I'd appreciate it if you'd fetch him for me."

His eyes shifted in the direction of the stables to see whether he could spot Nathan. Mary Ellen studied him and immediately something struck her that caused her discomfort as her face depicted a look of concern mixed with distrust.

"I'll get him."

She clutched the sides of her dress and ran toward the direction of the schoolhouse. Upon her arrival, she was nearly out of breath. She sucked wind as she prepared to speak.

Nathan's eyes depicted a sense of alarm from her behavior. "What is it? What's the matter?" He immediately stopped working and placed his hands around her arms.

She drew a deep breath. "There's a man here to see you. He said his name is Dusty. Didn't you mention someone named Dusty before?"

Nathan's eyes enlarged as he released her arms and quickly proceeded from the schoolhouse to where Dusty was standing beside his steed. Mary Ellen's countenance depicted danger as she grabbed the sides of her dress and bolted after Nathan.

She desired to hear their conversation and drew nearer. She wasn't satisfied so she stood beside Nathan.

Dusty spoke, "I believe I got a lead on those men that murdered your folks. There's a group of bandits that we got wind of that's been going around committing the same vicious acts."

Mary Ellen and Nathan's eyes enlarged. She turned toward Nathan and entreated him. "No no Nathan! You mustn't do this! Oh God please don't let him do this."

Nathan's eyes intensified and his breathing increased as he looked upon Dusty. It was as if Mary Ellen didn't exist as he completely disregarded what she said. Dusty continued, "Now I know that you said you didn't feel comfortable about doing this. But I've got a strong lead on these fellas and thought you'd reconsider hiring us."

Nathan inquired firmly, "What was their last position?"

Mary Ellen grabbed his arm and bellowed, "Nooo! Please don't do this Nathan. Don't do this to us!" She sobbed hard as her body shook and tears streamed down her face to her neck. She turned toward Dusty who acted nonchalant as he desired to get paid.

Dusty responded, "Now I can't give away their whereabouts without getting my fee."

Nathan responded with steely eyes, "Let's head over to the carriage house."

Mary Ellen cried out and gestured as she waved her hands forcefully in a downward motion, "Nathan we're finished! Don't you dare touch me anymore! Don't come around me anymore! Stay away from me! Don't you dare say another word to me and don't come anywhere near me!" Her body trembled as she vociferated, "Ever!"

Afterwards, Mary Ellen ran inside the mansion up the stairs to her room, slammed the door, and flung her body across her bed. She wasn't certain if anyone heard her and didn't care. She snatched the silk-tied cross from her neck that he had whittled for her, proceeded through the double-doors of her verandah, and tossed it to the ground. Afterwards, she returned inside and sobbed until her throat became sore. Her eyelids were puffy and her eyes were red.

She whimpered herself to sleep. Mary Ellen remained in her room the balance of the day. Marva knocked at her bedroom door just before supper to see whether she was alright.

She spoke to Marva with the door closed. "I'm not feeling well."

Marva insisted as she loved her little sister and had great respect for her. She leaned against the door and spoke, "Little Stockings please let me come inside so that we can talk. You didn't show up for supper last night or tonight. Let me come in."

She knocked persistently until Mary Ellen sat up and spoke hoarsely, "Alright, you can come in."

Marva looked at her face and eyes and immediately closed the door so that Mae wouldn't come in and start her tale bearing. Marva's eyes enlarged as she looked upon her younger sister.

"Girl what's going on? Did you and Nate have a fistfight or something? You look a sight!"

Mary Ellen flopped down on her bed, covered her face with her hands, and started sobbing all over again. Marva sat beside Mary Ellen and hugged her. "I don't get it. Everything was going so well with you yesterday. Tell me what happened."

Mary Ellen sniffed and wiped her face with her hand. "It's over between us." She nodded her head sideways in disgust. "He's never going to be saved. In fact, he's never going to amount to anything in the direction that he's headed in."

Marva didn't know what to make of what she said as a look of bewilderment shrouded her. "That was the same mistake that I made with Robert. You can't become involved with these unsaved men and think that their feelings for you is going to save their souls."

She looked steadily at Mary Ellen. "Only the Lord can save a soul. We can bat our eyelashes at them and pretty ourselves up. But only Jesus can save them honey."

Mary Ellen listened attentively as Marva continued with her southern accent, "I know what I'm talking about. You see what happened between me and Robert. Although Robert wasn't even an esquire like Nate. He didn't have any manners and he was a whoremonger. I nearly cried my eyes out on the rear verandah. But you see I ain't crying no more 'cause God wiped away my tears."

Mary Ellen hugged her sister. Marva consoled her.

"Are you hungry? I can have Miss Beatrice to fix you a plate and I'll have Miss Edna to bring it up 'cause if I do it, Big Mae might try to follow me up here to see what's going on. You gotta eat something."

Mary Ellen nodded in agreement and they hugged again. Marva got up and eased out of the door. Within approximately twenty minutes, Miss Edna tapped lightly at the door and announced herself. She was dressed in her maid's attire that consisted of a long black dress with a white apron and a matching white ruffled cotton mob cap. She spoke softly, "Little Stockings, it's me—Edna. I brought you some supper."

Mary Ellen eased her door open to ensure that Mae hadn't followed. She reached for the tray of food while being careful to keep her head lowered so that Miss Edna wouldn't become overly concerned and go get Mama Mae.

"Thank you."

"You're welcome and if you'd like, you can slide the tray outside the door when you're finished because I'll be up in about a half hour to fetch it."

Mary Ellen didn't realize how hungry she had become as she had been focused on how heartbroken she felt. She didn't leave any food or drink remaining.

She eyed the doors leading to the verandah and desperately desired to step outside. She chose to remain inside at least until dark because she didn't want to see Nathan; especially with her bad appearance and swollen eyelids.

Chapter Fifteen

Nathan nervously paced across the room as he wrung his hands. His heart pounded while beads of perspiration appeared on his face. His breathing intensified. He snatched glances through his window in the general direction of Mary Ellen's bedroom verandah. He realized that he'd made a mistake!

His pacing ceased as he positioned his body against the window. Tears flowed down his cheeks. He sniffed and wiped his face with his hand. His shoulders began to droop as his head lowered in shame.

He turned, grabbed some items, and ran quickly toward the stables. Within minutes, Nathan had exited the stables with Midnight. He mounted and then released a loud, "Yaw!" He rode Midnight toward the direction where Dusty had recently departed.

Nathan had finally caught up with Dusty. Dusty quickly drew his rifle not realizing that it was Nathan and fired a shot that caused him to fall off Midnight. Nathan didn't move while lying on the ground.

Dusty quickly dismounted his steed, ran over toward Nathan, stooped, and rolled him over. He was disappointed to see that he had shot Nathan. While nearly out of breath Nathan spoke slowly as he grasped Dusty's arm taut. "Wait! I don't want to do this." He sucked wind and continued, "I was coming to stop you. I don't want to...."

Dusty spoke and he examined the wound, "I'm so sorry. You took me by surprise and I didn't figure it would be you following me."

Nathan nodded his head slowly. "This is all wrong. It wasn't supposed to end this way."

Dusty realized that the bullet had grazed his arm. He removed Nathan's neckerchief and bound his wound.

"How bad is it?" Nathan's eyes focused heavily on Dusty's.

Dusty released a sigh of relief. "You're gonna be alright son. My bullet just licked your arm. I'm glad you weren't any closer, 'cause I'd uh probably done killed ya."

Nathan's eyes widened as he responded, "Licked! It hurts!" He squeezed his eyes taut for a second and then relaxed them as he was in pain from the sting of the wound.

"Just lie here while I fetch you something for the pain." Dusty got up and walked to his horse. He fumbled through some compartments of a leather bag strapped to his horse's bridle and retrieved a small vial.

He kneeled over Nathan who had sat up by himself. "Here drink some of this. It'll take away the pain."

Nathan's brows arched as he eyed the vial in disgust. "What is this stuff?"

"Laudanum!" He blocked it with his other hand and sneered.

A puzzled look appeared on Dusty's face as his brows furrowed. "Don't you want something for the pain?"

Nathan explained as he slowly eased himself up from the ground. "My father warned me a long time ago never to drink that stuff! He said it was addictive. He's seen many of men's lives ruined by that stuff!"

Dusty lowered his brows and responded, "I ain't never had a problem with this; although I have heard stories of other men that did. I mean I don't make it a regular part of my daily life and don't care to." He removed his cowboy hat, scratched his scalp, and placed his hat back on his head.

Nathan smirked again and then explained, "Before you shot me, I was on my way here to stop you from going after those men that you told me about. Just keep the down payment that I paid you for your trouble."

Dusty walked over to his steed and returned the vial to the leather compartment. Afterwards, he looked onward at Nathan as his brows rose while he spoke slowly. "Are you sure you want to end this?"

Nathan focused on him and responded sternly, "Yes!" He mounted his horse without using his sore arm. Their steeds faced one another.

"Alright. But you can't say I didn't try."

Nathan concluded before Dusty rode away. "Say Dusty, there's no need for you to come around these parts anymore."

Surprisingly, Dusty tossed him his money sack. Nathan caught it. "I don't accept wages for nothing. My daddy taught me to earn my money."

Nathan smiled, "I suppose we both had wise fathers."

A grin appeared on Dusty's face. "Have that nice looking young filly that's back there waiting for you to dress that arm of yours."

Nathan turned Midnight toward the direction of Beauford Place and released a loud, "Yaw!"

Nathan was greatly relieved that he had stopped Dusty although he didn't know how to reconcile his relationship with Mary Ellen. He wasn't certain as to whether she would be willing to accept any type of apology or explanation from him at this point because he didn't keep his word. Nathan regretted having let her down. As of now, he was too tired physically and mentally to do anything about the situation. Nathan had to stop and water Midnight on the way back. He knew that he had to think of some way to try to win Mary Ellen back. In the interim, upon his arrival to Beauford Place, he stopped by to see Mr. Pope.

"Ouch!" Nathan emitted loudly, while Mr. Pope cleaned and dressed his wound.

"Aw, that was just a little sting. You're good as new. Now tell me what happened that caused you to get shot and who did the shooting."

Nathan raised his eyes in disgust as he released a sigh. "Mr. Pope, it's probably best that you don't know. It was by accident anyway. I was riding my horse and another rider turned around and shot me in the arm. I'm just glad that I wasn't closer."

Mr. Pope paused a moment. "You can't go riding up on other riders without making certain that they know you're coming. You probably rode in such a way that made him think that you were somebody trying to do him harm."

Nathan looked up at Mr. Pope who was standing as he nodded in agreement. "Come to think of it, I was riding pretty hard. I had my mind on so many things."

Mr. Pope poured some coffee. "You know better than to do something stupid like that! You could've been killed. Did it have something to do with that fella that stopped by to see you earlier?"

Nathan squinted in surprise. "How did you know that and how did you see him?"

Mr. Pope sipped his hot coffee and chuckled. "First of all, I'm older. And I don't have anything better to do than to be nosey."

They laughed. Mr. Pope regained his composure and continued. "I don't believe that these eyes of mine miss a trick. And I'll tell you something else. Don't mess up a good thing. You got a chance to be with the woman of your dreams. You might not get a second chance at a woman like Mary Ellen."

His countenance took on a firm appearance as he responded regretfully, "I know. It might be too late to try and patch things up and I don't know if there's a chance that she'll ever forgive me. I'm so used to being a lone star. If only I hadn't been so selfish instead of caring about how she felt."

Mr. Pope gave his shoulder a manly pat and then sat across from him. "We all make mistakes son. It's probably not too late. You just need to make up your mind that this is what you want and the way you want to live. You know that you're gonna have to make some changes—changes that you might not be comfortable in making."

Nathan nodded in agreement as he sat with his fingers clasped. He pursed his lips for a second and spoke. "Well, it's getting latish. I guess I'll go to my quarters and think this through. Thanks for taking care of my arm for me."

He stood, pivoted, and proceeded toward the door. He heard Mr. Pope reply, "No problem, it was easy as licking butter from a knife." He rubbed his forehead and continued, "Now don't leave here and go being lunk-headed."

Nathan chuckled and gave a downward wave toward Mr. Pope as he departed.

Mary Ellen had cracked the door open to determine whether anyone was in the corridor so that she could slip the tray outside unnoticed. She did her best to be circumspect.

Marva's visit to her bedroom earlier helped to ease her discomfort. At least her crying had ceased. She repositioned herself on the side of her bed and gently soothed the aching pain from her head while rubbing her thumbs in a circular motion near her temples.

Mary Ellen heard footsteps creeping up the staircase and then she heard a faint sound of someone retrieving the dinner tray. An expression of relief appeared on her face as she didn't want any of the others to see the tray and get any notion to disturb her.

A few minutes later, she heard someone approaching and a faint knock at her door. "Little Stockings, it's me again."

Mary Ellen responded in a low tone, "Come in."

Marva entered and sat down beside her. She placed her arm on her little sister's shoulder to console her again. Mary Ellen noticed a look of sincerity in her eyes that she hadn't seen before. It was then that she realized that her sister really did love her.

"I'm glad that you were able to eat a little something."

She responded, "A little something! I felt as if I could have eaten the dishes too!"

They chuckled as their eyes twinkled and shoulders bounced rhythmically. They stopped their laughter briefly and then resumed laughing again.

"It's good to see you laugh," Marva spoke as she blotted her wet eyelids with the side of her finger.

Mary Ellen smiled with her lips closed. Afterwards, she spoke. "You know I've been thinking. I've had some time to really think things through being closed up in this room."

Marva interrupted, "Now don't plan to go do anything hasty."

Mary Ellen raised her right hand midway and continued, "Now let me finish what I have to say. I've been doing some thinking and I arrived at the conclusion that whatever has transpired between Nathan and I is in the past and I'm prepared to go on with my future. I'm a teacher and that's what I'm going to do. I'll teach at Beauford Place as planned and go on with my life."

Marva inquired, "How do you plan to deal with Nate working here while you stay here and teach?"

Mary Ellen's eyes became glossy, "I don't know. I do know this. I must forgive him and treat him like I treat the other workers. I'm friendly towards them and respectful and I'll treat him with the same friendliness and respect."

She knew in her heart that this wasn't going to be an easy task for her as Marva had began to explain, "Bear in mind, that it's not the same as Robert and me because I don't have to face Robert like you have to face Nate being here all day working around Beauford Place and sometimes maybe joining us for supper. Robert won't be coming around here anymore. In fact, it wouldn't surprise me to know that Robert's probably over some woman's house as we speak."

This was something for Mary Ellen to take under consideration. Marva continued to explain. "You need to understand that there will be times when you might look at him and still have feelings for him."

Mary Ellen stared blankly and replied, "I know. I realize—I wish that I had never allowed myself to become involved with him. I started not to from the beginning. But I let my emotions get the better of me."

Marva gave her hand a gentle pat. "Now don't go blaming yourself. Nate's very charming and handsome. I could see how easy it would be to fall in love with him."

She interrupted, "Yes but, when he didn't have his mind made up from the beginning—that should have served as an immediate warning to me not to become involved. But no, I just had to succumb to temptation. And just think, I judged you for succumbing to Robert and now I'm here in a mess!"

Marva's brows rose. "Are you telling me that you and Nate...."

When Mary Ellen saw the expression on Marva's face, she immediately knew what she was thinking and quickly interjected, "No! That's not what I'm talking about. I'm talking about falling in love! I shouldn't have allowed myself to fall in love. We didn't do anything else. I mean he kissed me gently at times and that was very brief because I wasn't going to allow it to go beyond that."

Marva's eyes resumed their normal state as she emitted a sigh of relief. "Thank God. You know mama would've hit the ceiling. It was bad enough when I was sleeping around with Robert. But with you, somehow I think her reaction would be more than any of us would be willing to put up with."

Mary Ellen smirked. "I know—I know. Because she and daddy had placed such high expectations for me to set the proper example as to how a lady should conduct herself in the Beauford family." She continued with a hint of sarcasm, "What an honor to bestow upon me!"

This time Marva sided with her parents' expectations. "I think that you're looking at this the wrong way. You don't see what I see. You've been a good example to me and Big Mae."

Mary Ellen's eyes began to tear as she spoke as best that she could while sobbing at the same time. "You have no idea as to what it's like to be me. I had to earn higher grades than anyone because of my parents' high expectations. I had to excel in all areas of my life because of my parents' high expectations."

She stood up and walked around the room like a prima donna. "I have to walk like a lady, talk like a lady, use proper manners, and be little miss perfect at all times even when I don't feel like it because of my parents' high expectations!"

Finally she stopped and pointed her finger at Marva who remained seated. "Let me tell you something, it's not easy being me! Everyone's always watching me—even at church because everyone expects me to excel in everything that I do!"

Marva sighed and stood in front of her as her countenance took on a serious expression. "Little Stockings, you are good at excelling in all that you do. You may not want to hear this, but it's the truth. And when you think about it after you calm down, you'll realize that

I'm speaking the truth. Ever since you were little, you were always good at what you do. It's who you are. You need to realize that you're special. Nate realized it because he sure didn't take notice towards me or any of the young sisters from church that would drop by for a visit every so often. And if you want to know the truth about that, me and Big Mae believe that they were just coming to see if they could get Nate to notice them."

Mary Ellen's eyes widened and she resumed her seated position. "Do you honestly think that they were coming to see Nathan?"

Marva reared her shoulders back with a look of astonishment as her mouth flung open. "Girl let me explain something to you. You see how they've been after Brother Trotter don't you?"

Mary Ellen nodded in agreement as her sister continued. "Well they used to come here and flaunt themselves at Nate and he showed his manners because that's the type of man that he is. But that's all the attention that he would show them. Nate doesn't strike me as the type of man that likes for women to flaunt themselves at him. He strikes me as being the type of man that likes to pursue the woman that he wants and I think that's what struck his fancy when he met you. You didn't throw yourself at him. You always carried yourself like a lady."

This pleased Mary Ellen as she smiled. Although she reminded herself that it was too late for her to consider having a future with Nathan at this point.

"I just wish that things had turned out differently for us. I did want to marry him and now he's gone off and probably gotten himself into some trouble with the law by now."

Marva's brows hunched. "What are you talking about?"

Mary Ellen drew a deep breath and nodded her head sideways. "It's a long story and I don't feel like going into it now. Anyway, you'll probably hear about it later or read about it in the newspaper."

This intrigued Marva even the more and she was determined not to retire for the evening until she uncovered the truth of the matter.

"Little Stockings, what is it that you're not telling me?"

Mary Ellen emitted a large sigh of frustration. "Nathan's parents were ministers and they were murdered right in front of him."

Marva's eyes widened. "What!"

She tapped Marva's hand. "Shhh. Keep your voice down. The only one that knew about this was daddy! Nathan had been saving his wages to hire some agency to track down the killers and he had been planning to kill the men instead of letting justice prevail."

Marva gasped, "What!" Afterwards, she quickly placed her hand over her mouth and replied, "Sorry. Go ahead."

Mary Ellen continued to explain, "A man stopped by to see him this morning from the agency and I suppose he gave Nathan the information as to the killers' whereabouts and the man doesn't know that Nathan plans to kill them instead of allowing him to make an arrest."

Marva lowered her hand from her mouth as her mouth flung open. Mary Ellen quickly repositioned Marva's hand back to cover her mouth.

"So you see that's why I let him know that I didn't want to have anything to do with him anymore. I can't marry an outlaw. Besides, I'm afraid that he might get himself killed and even if he doesn't that man from the agency will know that Nathan is the one that killed the men."

Marva did her best to squeeze out a response. "And he might have to track Nate this time. Oh no. Little Stockings you should have told mama or Mr. John. He would've told mama. Nate needs to be stopped before he messes up his life. We need to pray. Mama would send Mr. John after him to try and talk some sense to him."

Mary Ellen nodded her head in disagreement. "No don't tell mama. I tried several times to talk him out of it and I let him know that he wouldn't be able to have me if this is what he planned to do. He wouldn't listen and he's determined in his heart that this is what he wants to do. So I don't want to involve anyone else in this and possibly place their lives in danger. Nathan is a grown man and he knows exactly what he's doing."

This bit of news was more than what Marva had anticipated hearing. She was faced with a decision to either trust God or inform the family concerning the recent events.

She continued to sit next to Mary Ellen in deep thought. "I don't know what to do at this point except pray. You don't want to tell the family and I don't want to go behind your back and tell."

Mary Ellen explained as best that she could despite showing feelings of resilience and frustration as she slowly spoke. "Believe me. I have prayed day and night for him. I can do no more. If God doesn't do it at this point, nobody can. It's in God's hands now. We can do no more except have faith. It's starting to get late in the evening and we need to get prepared to attend church service in the morning."

Marva was seated in deep thought with her chin propped against her right hand until she finally decided to release it. "I guess you're right. You know more about the situation than I do. I had no idea that he had been struggling with this. He never showed any signs that anything was bothering him. I guess that old saying is true.

You never know what a person is thinking on the inside or what's in a person's heart. "

She turned toward Mary Ellen. "Let me ask you something before I go. Did you think that you could change him or that his feelings for you were somehow going to change him?"

Despite her embarrassment, Mary Ellen answered honestly. "Yes. I did."

Marva pursed her lips and responded gently. "I thought so. That was the same mistake that I made with Robert. Like I said earlier, only God can save their souls."

Mary Ellen concluded before Marva exited the door, "And only God can change the heart and minds of mankind."

Marva turned and nodded in agreement as she quietly closed the door behind her.

Mary Ellen changed her attire, climbed into bed, and was finally able to relax and be at peace as she quickly drifted into a deep slumber.

Chapter Sixteen

SUNDAY MORNING

The Beauford household scurried about as they prepared themselves to be ready in time to attend church service. Marva had ensured that Mary Ellen was up and about. No one stayed home from church in the Beauford mansion unless they were ill or an emergency existed.

Mary Ellen sat in front of her vanity and was glad to see that her eyes were relieved of most of the swelling. She got up, walked over to her wardrobe, and slid dresses across the clothes rod. She retrieved a lovely fuchsia colored dress with sleeves made of fabric roses. She told herself that it was too cheerful looking and immediately returned it to the wardrobe. She chose a bluish-green dress and draped it across her bed. She resumed her seated position at her vanity, reached inside the drawer, retrieved a necklace set, and placed it next to the fabric to determine a match.

Mary Ellen blew her breath in frustration as she grabbed her hair because it looked terrible in the looking-glass. Nonetheless, she knew an old trick to make it look presentable as she planned to wear a large wide-brimmed hat with matching plumage. She cornrowed her thick hair until it resembled a broided crown.

After getting dress, Mary Ellen eased down the stair case in anticipation of facing the morning. Upon reaching the stoop, she was immediately interrupted by Big Mae who stood poised with her hands upon her oversized hips. She spoke in a signifying tone, "What's been going on with you lately? You didn't show up for supper. Nobody's heard a peep out of you. What you got a case of the women's monthly blues? Are you on the rag or something?"

Mary Ellen did her utmost to remain calm. She was not up to dealing with another one of Big Mae's shenanigans today much less her prying.

Mary Ellen sidestepped her and proceeded to the front verandah to see who their driver was this morning and was relieved to see that it was Mr. John. She seated herself on the swing until everyone was ready. Mary Ellen had hoped that she didn't have to ride with Big Mae. But she didn't have any choice this morning. She proceeded to the carriage and Mr. John assisted her. "Good morning Mr. John."

"Good morning Little Stockings. I missed seeing you and Nate at the supper table last night."

She smiled at him and didn't respond. Afterwards, she heard some raucous which was none other than her loud-talking sister Big Mae, who walked as if she was bouncing her hips toward the carriage. She purposely tried to squeeze in beside Mary Ellen until she squealed, "Girl, why don't you climb in the next seat and stop trying to sit next to me! You know that the only reason that you want to sit up here is to pester me and be nosey."

Big Mae smiled as Mr. John regretted having to assist her. He spoke up, "Where's lazy Jack?"

Mary Ellen laughed.

Big Mae explained as she tried to sound ladylike, "Oh he's feeling a bit under the weather this morning so he won't be joining us today."

Mr. John responded, "I'll bet he is after dealing with you."

Mary Ellen laughed again. She was grateful for Mr. John's witty banter. He knew how to get things stirred up and create a bout of laughter.

Marva proceeded toward the carriage as she closed the wrought-iron gate behind her. She climbed in and seated herself next to Mary Ellen who preferred her company in place of Big Mae's any day. Mr. John ensured that everyone was secure and proceeded in the direction of the church.

After riding a bit, Big Mae just had to get started. "So as I was asking you earlier, why didn't I see you at supper last night?"

Before Mary Ellen could respond, Marva interjected. "Big Mae shut up and mind your own business!"

Big Mae smirked. "I was just showing my concern. Why can't I make polite conversation on the way to church?"

Marva looked back and gave her a contemptible sneer. "I said mind your own business! And you know full well that you're not trying to make polite conversation. You're just trying to find something to gossip about because you don't have anything going on that satisfies you in your life with Jack."

She adjusted her millinery and retorted, "Yes I do. I have a husband."

This time, Mary Ellen and Marva turned around and stared at Big Mae. Mr. John had taken a glance with a look of disgust.

Big Mae exclaimed, "What's wrong with Jack?"

No one responded as they resumed their positions.

Mary Ellen nodded her head sideways and then she massaged the sides of her head with her thumbs again. Mary Ellen looked at Marva and spoke, "I think that I should have done what Jack did this morning and stayed home. I really don't feel like being annoyed this morning."

Mary Ellen winced at Marva and spoke, "Big Mae's just disappointed that we decided not to share our secret with her."

This piqued Big Mae's attention as she repositioned herself attentively. "What secret are you talking about? Let me hear it. What's going on?"

Marva and Mary Ellen turned around and replied, "No!"

Big Mae chuckled, "You too are just kidding around. There's no secret. Is there?" Her brows rose.

Marva and Mary Ellen glanced at her and then at one another and burst into a bout of laughter.

Big Mae developed a bad attitude and refused to speak to them the remainder of their journey to church.

Mary Ellen was careful not to allow herself to be seated next to Brother Lawrence Trotter. She's been that way ever since that day he decided to pay her a visit at Beauford Place. She simply wanted to focus on the sermon, as she desired a spiritual uplift. The choir had a second selection to sing.

She blotted her eyes while they began to sing, as it was one of her favorite hymnals. Marva gave her back a gentle rub as she was seated behind her. Mary Ellen glanced over her shoulder and whispered, "Thank you."

She expanded her fan, as it was warm. She fanned herself and enjoyed the singing as it soothed her heart. After the collection plate had been passed around, she knew that the reading of Scripture was next. She prepared to stand as the minister had beckoned with his hands for the congregation to stand.

Mary Ellen listened attentively to the words of the passage of Scripture.

Blessed is the man that endureth temptation: for when he is tried, he shall receive the crown of life, which the Lord hath promised to them that love him. James 1:12

She was glad to see Bishop Bronnum approach the pulpit. After he opened with prayer he began his sermon with two Scriptures.

He staggered not at the promise of God through unbelief;
but was strong in faith, giving glory to God;

And being fully persuaded that, what he had promised, he
was able also to perform. Romans 4:20-21

Mary Ellen listened attentively as Bishop Bronnum
delivered his sermon. She knew that she lacked the faith to
stand on some of God's promises although it was her
intention to be strong. She realized that she wasn't as
strong as she had believed herself to be.

As he continued preaching, she felt Marva tap her
shoulder. She turned her head slightly to see what Marva
wanted. Marva pointed toward the rear.

Mary Ellen's eyes widened and her mouth gaped as
she observed Nathan sitting on the last pew dressed up in
one of her father's Sunday suits. Seated beside him was
Mama Mae who winced at Mary Ellen. Nathan had driven
Mama Mae to church.

He looked very handsome and distinguished. What
truly drew her attention was the fact that he resembled the
painting of her late father. She glanced at him a second
time and observed him holding a Bible and following along
as his attention was focused toward the direction of the
pulpit.

Mary Ellen drew a deep breath as she listened to the
sermon concerning God's faithfulness to His promises. She

felt Marva reach over and squeeze her gloved hand. Mary Ellen tried to remain poised, as she didn't want to draw unnecessary attention to herself.

After Bishop Bronnum concluded his sermon, he made an altar call for sinners to come for prayer to receive salvation. Mary Ellen dared not to look back a third time. She held her breath for a moment until she observed Nathan approach the altar and kneel.

Bishop Bronnum anointed him with oil, talked with him for a while, and then prayed hard for him. Nathan raised his hands as tears flowed. Mary Ellen raised her hands and rejoiced in the Lord while her eyes welled with tears. Everyone could hear Mama Mae as she rejoiced in the Lord along with the other parishioners.

Afterwards, everyone witnessed Nathan's baptism. When Bishop Bronnum immersed him in the water, everyone rejoiced and many danced around the church as the choir sang baptismal hymnals. Marva hugged Mary Ellen and then Mae walked over and hugged her while a smile stretched across Jack's face. Mary Ellen couldn't hug her mother because Mama Mae still danced around and rejoiced. Mr. John and Mr. Pope were extremely happy. Miss Beatrice and Miss Edna rejoiced.

After church service had ended, the family and staff returned to Beauford Place. Nathan stood on the front verandah and stared in Mary Ellen's eyes as they were still dressed in their Sunday attire. He kneeled on one knee, reached for her hand, and looked upward at her. "Mary Ellen Beauford, will you please marry me?"

She smiled heartily and bounced somewhat. "Yes. I will."

He stood and drew her to him and graciously kissed her and then she asked, "What happened to your plans?"

He looked at her with his striking eyes and replied, "I couldn't go through with it. I talked to your mother because I was scheduled to drive her to church this morning. I told her everything. I told her that I just couldn't do it. She took me inside and gave me one of your father's suits—actually, she said that I could have all of them including his cowboy hat and anything else of his that I desired. I told her how much you meant to me and she invited me to church and she waited for me to get cleaned up." He sighed. "It feels good to finally be rid of that burden. I'm free now."

Mary Ellen hugged him. "I'm so glad."

She looked up at him. "Do you mind moving to the mansion after we're married because I don't want to live in the carriage house?"

He lifted her chin and answered, "I don't mind at all," and gave her a kiss that caused her millinery to fall on the verandah—they didn't care.

Mary Ellen stood on the freshly mowed lawn dressed in an exquisite Victorian styled high-buttoned neck white wedding gown. Her hair was pressed and styled in a Victorian bouffant coiffure. She wore matching white lace fingerless gloves and pearl clip-on earrings. On her ring finger sat a large diamond with a gold band that Nathan purchased with the money that he had saved.

She held a large mixed bouquet arrayed with colorful flowers as she was about to become Mrs. Nathan Jonah Hickey. She clutched the wooden necklace that he carved for her. Mr. John had found it lying in the grass and returned it to her. Her sisters stood alongside her dressed in lovely pink flowing dresses and matching millinery. Mama Mae's pink dress and millinery matched theirs. She also wore a lovely fresh corsage. The lawn was filled with townspeople, their church family, and family members including the loud, obnoxious, and drunken ones.

Nathan was dressed in a black tailored tuxedo. Mr. John, Mr. Pope, and Jack stood alongside them dressed similar to Nathan. Mr. John had given Mary Ellen away. After they had spoken their vows, Bishop Bronnum announced that he could kiss her.

Nathan gave Mary Ellen a kiss like never before now that they were married that nearly knocked her off her feet. Her eyes enlarged and she drew a deep breath as he peered into her doleful eyes and spoke, "I love you Mrs. Hickey," while Uncle Addison nearly temporarily blinded them from snapping pictures.

They didn't desire to travel anyplace. Therefore, Mama Mae had a large bedroom prepared for them as well as the east wing of the mansion to afford them privacy. Nathan escorted her to the east wing of the mansion, carried her across the threshold, and closed the door to their new oversized bedroom complete with new furnishings, which were wedding gifts from Mama Mae. She had an extra bedroom furnished as a sitting room to afford them additional privacy.

Nathan and Mary Ellen stood on the verandah outside of their new bedroom around midnight dressed in their robes and stared up at the sky. He held her in his arms as they gave thanks to God. Afterwards, he kissed her and spoke, "It's hard for me to believe that you're my wife."

Dr. Mary Ellen Beauford-Hickey received numerous accolades throughout the years as she became nationally renowned as an African-American teacher that paved the way for disadvantaged youths to achieve an education. *The Benjamin Beauford Schoolhouse* eventually enlarged and became *The Benjamin Beauford College* as they received approval years later to expand it into a private college.

Mama Mae appointed Nathan as the overseer of the ranch as he loved being a cowboy. She also appointed him and Mary Ellen to assume the head seating positions at the dining table in place of her and Benjamin as she had her Will revised to appoint them over Beauford Place in the event of her demise. Nathan also became an associate minister at church.

Mary Ellen and Nathan remained together throughout their tests and trials—throughout the good and tough times. They never regretted their decision to marry as their love for one another remained constant because they placed their faith and trust in the Lord Jesus.

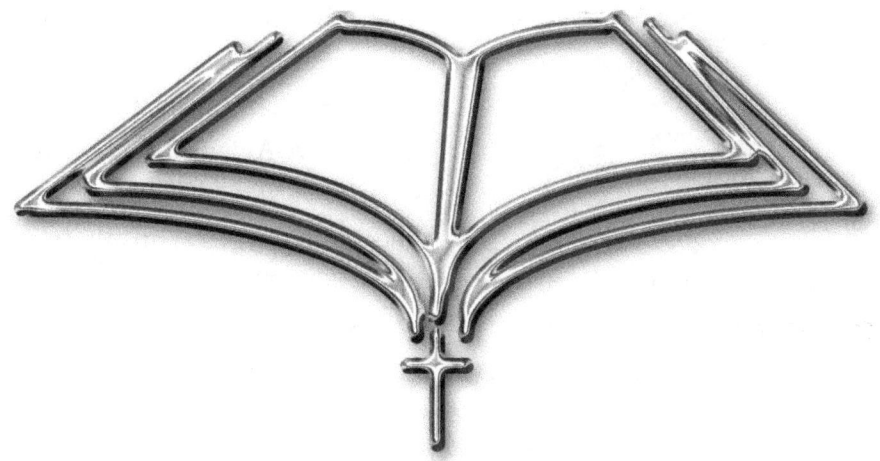

Gwandine has enjoyed writing since childhood when she would create stories, make miniature books from construction paper, and draw the illustrations for the covers. She is a canvas painter and former porcelain doll sculptress. Gwandine's paintings depict African-American cowboys and Native-Americans as she is of Cherokee and African descent. She enjoys writing inspirational parables and non-fictional spiritual books to help those on their journey with Jesus. Gwandine also writes and illustrates her graphic novels depicting her characters.

She has toured and exhibited in the U.S. and has donated African-American figurative sculptures for permanent exhibit in the Afro-American Museum and Cultural Center. She serves as a pastor and is married to a pastor. They have two adult children. Gwandine believes that the Lord Jesus has blessed and inspired her in this endeavor.

Should you desire additional information, please visit:

GWANDINE.com
Other books available by Gwandine are:

A Place in the Wilderness – Exodus to Cimarron City
The Ethiopian Princess and the Cameroon Knight
Weight Management and Daily Devotional

The Cowboy, the Preacher, and the Lady
Powerful Kingdom Women Series
A Love Worth Finding
Mystery in Manalapan
Saints and Church Folk
In Whom Do I Trust?
Gwandine Magazine
The Anointed Atura
The Black West
Prairie Sisters
Mrs. Mystery
Poetic Peace
Xerzinia
Jade Qi

And if the Lord says the same, there will be more to come.

As always, I like to pray the Lord's blessings upon this book to bless and inspire all who read it. You too can have a love worth finding. I am not talking about a love that will let you down or disappoint you. I am talking about the Lord Jesus Christ. He will never leave nor forsake you. In reality, Jesus Christ is a love worth finding.

If you do not know Jesus in the pardon of your sins, you can begin by asking Him to forgive you for all your sins and to come into your life. Afterwards, pray and seek the Lord to lead you to a Bible believing full Gospel church so that you can be fed the Word of God. Then begin allowing Jesus to use you to lead others to Him.

Faithful and Holy is He!
Yours in Christ,

—Gwandine—

Published by Faithful and Holy is He! Studios and Productions

www.ingramcontent.com/pod-product-compliance
Lightning Source LLC
Chambersburg PA
CBHW071137170626
46809CB00002B/659